OLD GREENBOTTOM INN

AND OTHER STORIES

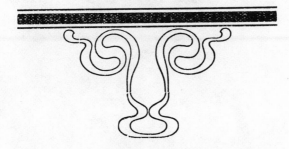

AMS PRESS

NEW YORK

OLD GREENBOTTOM INN.

OLD GREENBOTTOM INN
AND OTHER STORIES

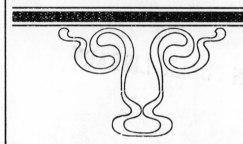

BY

GEORGE MARION McCLELLAN
LOUISVILLE
1906

Library of Congress Cataloging in Publication Data

McClellan, George Marion, 1860-
  Old Greenbottom Inn and other stories.

  Reprint of the 1906 ed. published in Louisville, Ky.
  CONTENTS: Old Greenbottom Inn.—For Annison's sake.
—A Creole from Louisiana. [etc.]
  1. Negroes—Fiction. I. Title.
PZ3.M13190l10 [PS3525.A155]   813'.5'2   74-144654
ISBN 0-404-00199-8

Reprinted from the edition of 1906, Louisville
First AMS edition published in 1975
Manufactured in the United States of America

AMS PRESS INC.
NEW YORK, N. Y. 10003

PROEM.

Τράγος, the goat; ὠδή, the song; and from this, "The Song of the Goat," and then the word tragedy. Perhaps the goat, as a prize for the best performance of that song in which the germs of future tragedy lay, or because the first actors in Bachinalian revelries dressed as Satyrs, in goat skins, gave the original idea of the thing the word embodies.

More probable, perhaps, the goat, a spoiler of vines, was a fit subject for sacrifice in a feast to Dionysus, a death song being sung in the while of slaughter, or what not. Out of this shadowy connection comes the word **tragedy,** with all its significance.

Aeschylus is at once put down as the father of tragedy, while the word itself makes us, first of all others, think of Shakespeare. With Aeschylus and Shakespeare in mind, a tragedy suggests to our minds only some dramatic representation of signal action, where some illustrious persons move in an event, or a series of events, which culminate at last in the loss of life by human violence.

Famous tragedies show us the unequal struggle of man against fate, and in this realm, those terrible struggles of King Lear, to the equal, but finer and more spiritual struggles of Hamlet—are simply those often seen in the most lowly life and commonplace events.

In such a case, the events, the inexorable environments and meshes through which the victim struggles, are too insignificant for notice in a conception of tragedy, and when the final catastrophe comes, the life lost, if noticed at all, is regarded only as a natural consequent of vulgarity, sin and a willful prostitution of life. All the groping in the dark, all of the victim's bitter struggle after the better self amid evil environments, where blind and contradictory forces led the way, are not taken in account when judgment is past.

Yet all the movements necessary to a great tragedy went on in due procession, where, in case of the illustrious, could have been seen sublime sorrow and grand crimes.

In the domain of the South, among its darker subjects, are many pitiable tragedies, not known by that name. By and by, that one from among us who is coming, who has not yet arrived, but whose heralds are already heard in the distance proclaiming his sure coming, will tell our stories. And then the great heart of all our vast domain, which ever responds to great sorrow when it is touched, and, notwithstanding its multitudinous contradictions, is ever working towards right and justice to all—will make many things better concerning which now exist only silence, unbelief and indifference,

CONTENTS.

––––––

OLD GREENBOTTOM INN.

"INDUSTRIAL AND MECHANICAL ARTS."—in large print above the door of the central work-shop. Under that sign in front of the door the band was playing "Manhattan Beach"—one of the gayest of Sousa's marches. There were a dozen or more students in various attitudes, sitting or standing on the rocks in front of the band. In groups of larger numbers others were slouching out of "Seay Hall" and "The Annex" towards the industrial work-shops. They were coming to "The Line." There would be roll-call in a few minutes and those furthest behind began to hasten their gait. Tardiness of minutes stretched into hours on the "Rock-pile." The Saturday afternoon drill began at four o'clock. It was an all-glorious afternoon, but old "Buck" and "Jerry" did not feel its poetry. They felt only the lash instead. As they rounded the corner by Palmer Hall old Jerry stumbled and fell to his knees. When he got on his feet again he stopped and old Buck stopped for company. "Go on you lazy rascils, you infernal beastes."

And with these words of tender address, across their bony backs Gillon laid the lash. With tongues out, and bowed heads, under yokes heavier than any the Romans ever laid upon the necks of the Jews, these two unpitied oxen began again their slow and measured pace. There was no resentment to the lash, except by the twitching of tails. And these were the symbols of patience? Patience never! They were the symbolization of dispair in the most helpless servitude. It was the old tread of slavery, in which there was no hope and no future except that of beating and thankless toil, which old Jerry and Buck symbolized as they slowly made their way up the hill with their heavy load of meal, barrels of pickled pork and of molasses to feed the hungry students. Up from the laundry with baskets, three girls came with heavy loads, but not hopelessly. They were bringing the teachers' clothes to "Turner Hall." Down from the hospital, wearing her white cap, came one of the nurses singing at the top of her voice—"I don't want to play in your yard, I don't like you any more," and with this defiant but joyful melody, headed off a more sorrowful band bound to the "Place of Correction." There were just seven in all coming out of Professor's office and two of them were weeping bitterly, while three others moved on with sulks. The other two had been in as witnesses. Notwithstanding the grieved faces they bore in Professor's office and the righteous indignation with which one of the two had said: "It's a shame, Perfesser, de way dat gal cussed we all," they were both giggling now. It was the five who were to be punished. Beyond Langston Hall in the quarry on the hillside there were twenty-eight boys pecking rock. They had led in the "Sweep" the night before in Seay Hall. There was a brief sitting of the faculty in the morning, and the verdict—"Seven days on the Rockpile at hard labor." Somehow the "Sweep" which had been such fun the night before seemed a very stupid affair as they remembered it out there in the quarry. Up by the big spring the anvils in the blacksmith shops were ringing merrily and there was a whirr of the broom factory overhead. In the distance there was the thrumming of pianos and the indistinct murmur of voices that belong to a boarding school. All over the campus and the halls and the workshops there was the busy and happy, swarming life of the Industrial and Normal school of four hundred negro students. The sweet

9

breath of May was everywhere and the outside was too lovely for me to remain indoors. I came out with my pencil and notebook and sat down to dreams on the soft grass by the band-stand. The line had formed and the roll-call was over. All slouch was gone now and it moved with precision on the hillside with soldierly bearing to the shouts of command of the officer in charge and the martial strains of music. Far to the south the ''Three Mountains,'' cone-shaped, made one think of the pyramids and the sands of Egypt. East of the ''Three'' Monte Sano, the highest and the pride of them all, lifted its head to views westward beyond the mountain districts of Northern Alabama to lovely lowlands stretching away towards the Mississippi. And to the west of Greenbottom Inn there were other mountains that seemed already lost in the coming dreams of evening. Down their sides the shadows were beginning to creep and the afternoon's robes of amethyst, which they so often wore, were slowly enfolding them. But in all the lovely valley towards Buena Vista, where the church spires went up white towards heaven, there was the soft sunshine of the afternoon, the green fields, the flowers and the glorious foretaste of summer. Just below at my feet, there was Greenbottom Inn, with all its jovial history, its poetry, its romance, its comedy and tragedy of slavery days. It was all there on the mountain sides and in all that little valley, woven in with the history of that once famous inn. I felt it all and saw it all, but I could not begin to write it down. To sit there in a dream of the past with all the stir of the present life in my ears and to give myself up wholly to sensations of mingled joy and sadness—sadness for what there had been and joy for what there was, was better than to write as I came out to do. Greenbottom Inn! Who would look at it now and connect it with its past? Now it is the "TEACHERS' HOME—NEGRO TEACHERS of the INDUSTRIAL and N O R M A L SCHOOL. Its kitchen and back yard have become the front side of the house, for the public road runs further up the hill now. And exactly the same change has taken place in the ownership and use of the old mansion. True, the old portico looks out upon the grassy lawn, the brick pavement, the row of box that once led to the front gate; for, after all, the old Inn is as set in its old tracks as are some of the "Sesesh" who once made its passing life in ante-bellum times. The old gate hangs on its rusty hinges and opens into the old road, long disused, but still there with worn stones and lasting footprints of the processions that have passed by. It was the old slave track, coming down from Virginia and North Carolina by the way of East Tennessee, over which many chain-gangs of slaves with broken hearts have passed to the Southern cotton plantations of Alabama and Mississippi. In the balmy air of the seductive afternoon, I sat there and watched them go by again with all their bitter tragedy of life and with none to write their names in the book of remembrance and to tell the generations to come their sorrows. I was aroused at last by the coming of a lad of eighteen—one of the seniors and head printer in the printing office. "Professor, here are the proofs of the programme for the vesper service." (Most of the students called me Professor, though that title belonged exclusively to the head of the school in a very peculiar sense in that little community.) "Isn't the scene lovely from here?" "Why don't you write some poetry on Buena Vista, Professor?" "I can't write poetry here," I replied. "The poetry all about me is too sublime to be praised in such verse as I

can write." "O, I think your poetry is
beautiful. " "Thank you. This proof is
all right. You had better get it back to
the printing office before the supper bell
rings. I see 'The Line' is disbanding:"
I liked this particular lad, and watching
his happy, youthful swing back to the
printing office, I repeated mentally: "He
is the worst boy in school." That was the
first thing I heard about him when I came
as teacher and chaplain. He was bad
enough I soon found out, but I found the
way to his good side, which was plenteous
also. His coming with the proof of the
Sunday evening service broke my dream
and aroused me to the sense of the things
around me. They were but the familiar
sounds and daily sights of the campus.
Still they filled me with a sense of unutterable pathos and brought a train of my earliest recollections—indeed the earliest recollections of mankind belonged to the
scene. The flocks were browsing along the
hillside and slowly wending their way to
the folds. The little lambs were bleating
with that fretful tone which belongs to little children when the night comes on. And
in the softer, but coarser, bleat of the old
sheep there was unmistakably the tender
tones of the mother. The lowing cows

from the upland pastures and low-lying meadows were coming home with their rich contributions to the family board. What ties there have ever been between the flocks, the herds, and the families further back than the most ancient civilization. The smoke was curling over the kitchen chimney of the Teachers' Home, heralding the supper. In a flash I saw Greenbottom Inn in all its glory of ante-bellum days, and a beautiful quadroon girl who used to watch the coming of the cows and meet them with milkmaid songs and caressing names.

"A beautiful, innocent child indeed! She's a nigger brat, and she'll bring disgrace and ruin along her track as her mother has done—as her mother did before her. I tell you once for all, John McBride, Lucinda and her brat shall go to the nigger trader, or I will go back to Kentucky." The quarrel was fierce and bitter between husband and wife. Both were determined, but the wife came off conqueror in part; for when John McBride left the house Lucinda's doom was sealed. He knew his wife would keep her word. He had no alternative. She would go to Kentucky and with her would go her money. Greenbottom Inn and the plantation were heavily mortgaged and John McBride's financial situation was precarious. Without the help of his wife's income, not only Lucinda, but all the negroes would, in a short time, go to the trader. Celia McBride knew that, and he ended the quarrel by saying: "You know you have me at your mercy; Lucinda will have to go." "And the brat, too," added the victorious wife. Then all the unconquerable will and fight of the McBrides, which had passed on from generation to generation with many bloody battles left on the records of the local feuds, found a true son in this innkeeper representative. "No, by God; the child shall not go—not to save you from going to hell, let alone Kentucky." Celia McBride knew that her victory covered the sale of Lucinda, and wisely decided to let the war end there. A little child—a wonderfully beautiful quadroon girl, had been by the doorway listening to the quarrel without understanding its import. She heard her mother's name called and vaguely felt in some way she was blamed, and she went from the door repeating the sentence—"She's a nigger brat." This saying she remembered long after the quarrel, and the terrible scene which she witnessed the next day had faded from her memory. The heat of the morning quarrel between husband and wife passed by, and life at the Inn went on as usual that day till late in the afternoon. When the sun was dipping low behind the mountains of the west, a long train of melancholy travelers drew up at the Inn, bringing to it the excitement that such a train always brought, though many such passed that way. Mrs. McBride had had notice of the traders coming, and when they drew up to the Inn at sunset, she was expecting them. She had waited their coming with secret exultation and nervous anxiety all day. There were three white men in the train—the two guards and the speculator, also two bloodhounds. The rest of the train were men, women and children, from the tents of Ham. The men were chained together by twos, and a few of the women were thus manacled, who had proved refractory at the setting out. The speculator drew up at the Inn with a jovial air. He prided himself upon being a good and merciful negro driver, and he was, as compared with many such who passed that way. The sight of the Inn, with the smoke curling over its kitchen chimney, the aroma of coffee, the savory scent of frying ham, that greeted him in the air, and the

16

mental vision of hot biscuits, such as only the South knows about, promised a supper close at hand that his soul delighted in. His good will towards all men rose up to the occasion. Besides, out there by the spring, where the camp was struck, with two white men on guard with rifles and bloodhounds, he had some wonderfully good bargains. Indeed, towards the northern borders of the slave-land, negroes were beginning to be cheap. Fred Douglass, Sojourner Truth (runaway slaves), Garrison, Wendell Phillips, and Harriet Beecher Stowe were stirring the pulse of the nation to a high fever. Away off in Kansas, John Brown was training a little band of men who were going to strike a blow at Harper's Ferry that was to shake the heart of the country through and through. By a a few, blood and carnage were already scented from afar. But old Jim Callahand, the speculator in slaves, comforted by Celia McBride's good supper and one more good bargain, was happy and blind to all things except the promises of the devil, to whose kingdom he belonged soul and body, though he was of the best of "nigger" drivers. He went to his bed with a feeling of peace and good will towards all the world and most satisfied with himself and his business qualities. The "nigger," Lucinda, had come cheap, so determined was the mistress that she should go with that melancholy gang, camping out by the spring. And that chain gang lay down to its rest also, but not with the peace of the master. They were so weary many of them went to sleep as soon as the camp was struck, and their coarse fare was eaten. With the coming of the evening shadows the heart of the world turns homeward, but theirs was a sorrowful coming of night, except for the short hours of sleep, for in else than that, they had no hope except in death. Most of them had come so far, were so utterly weary and benumbed at heart, there was no weeping. There was just that dumb-animal expression of pain, despair and anguish written on their faces for which there are no words in language to describe. After the supper was over at the Inn, Lucinda, on her way to her cabin, passed by the sorrowful camp at the spring and cast a look of unutterable pity on the poor wretches, little dreaming that on the morrow she would be one of their number. But that very night the price for her was paid, and though it was again the price of blood, her master who received it, went not out as Judas to hang himself, but before the dawn he did go out a man sore at heart to be far away when the slave train left the Inn. The girl, Lucinda, had been the passion of his boyhood with all the liberties that the times and the slave system permitted. There had been two boys who mercifully went out of this life soon after they got in it. After them there was a marriage that ought never to have been, though both were sincere and meant well in the beginning. John McBride knew lawful marriage and little Eunice came to seal the compact. For a while he was happy and Lucinda was forgotton. But the husband and wife were too unlike. There were little misunderstandings at first, silent broodings over wrongs by the one that the other never meant, never thought of. At times there was gross injustice on both sides until the war of silent scorning began, killing much that was best in both, and making all that which followed but the natural fruit of mistakes. Then in this era Lucinda was again remembered, and one day there came to the Inn the "nigger brat." Celia McBride was not naturally a mean and vindicative woman, but in hate and cruelty to which a jealous woman may go there is yet no limit fixed, and the greatest examples of cruelty that the world has to show

19

comes from the ranks of women. When the slave train prepared for its start Celia McBride stood with smiles in her doorway to enjoy her triumph over her fallen foe. Lucinda knew nothing of her sale till the hour before her departure. The scene was terrible. She fought like a tigress and raved like a maniac. She would not move one step with the slave train for all the oaths and beating of that merciful "nigger" driver. At last bleeding and torn, she was bound hand and foot in the luggage cart of the train. And the mistress looked on with pleasure at Lucinda's anguish till the bound negro put such a curse of death and ruin upon her and her house she turned with terror from the work she had wrought. And there came into her heart a great dread and fear that the curse of desolation and death which the bound tigress pronounced would come to pass. In time the curse did come to pass, for the time came when the heart of Celia McBride was desolate, when she went at last to the grave poor and lonely, and the old Inn went to strangers, and strangest of all, to Negroes. But Celia McBride was queen of the situation that morning when Lucinda went, bound with thongs, with the slave train. It left the Inn early that morning and as it

turned into the Meridian turnpike stretching as a white line to the south, it passed a
little child whose hand was held by a Negro
lad of ten years. She looked on the passing scene bewildered, hearing the screams
of the bound woman, and knew not that
she was her mother. And the mother bound
on her back in the cart, with her face turned to the pitiless sky, looking down on her
with blue smiles, knew not that she passed
by her child forever. But the Negro lad of
ten saw it all and understood it all. He
stooped and kissed the child, who wondered at this first caress. Then he tender-
ly took her in his arms and carried her to
the Inn. So soon was love come into his
heart that was to rend it in twain. Lucinda went her way to the far slave market at
Mobile. Whatever was her sorrowful life
and whatever became of her at last the
judgment day will only make known—that
is if on that day even, the wrongs put on so
many helpless Negro men and women will
be remembered and righted. When the
night came, on the day Lucinda was carried
away, after the supper was over, a little
child was weeping in the dark kitchen, forgotten by all the world at that hour. Celia
McBride heard the sobs, and at the sight of
the hated child so utterly forsaken, the

mother heart triumphed. She took her to
the room where her own child lay sleeping
in her soft bed and made a pallet for the
Negro child and put her to bed. This moth-
erly act was not without pity, but it was
aided by a secret remorse that the child
knew not of and which secured for her a
protection and a home from that very woman who had the day before clamored for her
sale to the Negro trader. One day a year
after the sale of Lucinda, the Inn was
again the scene of excitement. John Mc-
Bride rode up from Buena Vista with great
haste and announced the startling news,
that Fort Sumter had been fired upon.
Then the North and the South took up the
mighty cry of war. Not many days after,
John McBride took his knapsack and went
to the front to defend his country from the
invaders. In this hour of meeting a common foe, the husband and wife were again
united. Celia McBride took the reins of
the government at home and for a while
things went well at Greenbottom Inn. John
McBride was at the front in the thickest of
the battle, valiantly defending his fireside
and Southern altars. For a while both husband and wife were confident of victory
and so was all the South. Indeed, until the
middle of the third year of the war, things

were in a very doubtful state. The second
year closed with Jackson's splendid movements and victories in the Shennandoah
and Lee's triumph in the peninsular
against Pope. Bragg had made his famous
raid in Kentucky. The battle of Cedar
Mountains, Chickasaw Bluffs and Fredericksburg had all been gained by the Con-
federate soldiers. Lee well nigh made a
successful invasion of the north and was
planning to renew the attempt. Grant had
subdued the west and the subjugation of
the southwest was half done, but his victories did not offset those of the east. The
South was arrogant and confident of victory. Galveston had fallen into the hands
of the rebels, and thus a seaport was
opened. Burnsides had received a check
in his victories in East Tennessee. The
naval attack at Charleston had proved a
failure. Port Hudson was not then fallen
and Grant was still held at bay at Vicksburg. After the defeat of the Union soldiers
at Chancellorsville and Fredericksburg, at
one time they were deserting at the rate of
two hundred a day. Things for the Union
were critical and gloomy at the North. A
strong peace party had arisen there. The
draft for soldiers was very unpopular, and,
provoked by it, a riot broke out in New

York City which, for cold-blooded barbarity, the South has yet to produce a lynching to equal it. And so on to the first of July in the middle of the third year of the war did the promise of victory belong to the South. On the second day at Gettysburg, the South, represented by Gen. Lee, was confidently in a few days expecting in Philadelphia or New York to dictate terms of peace. But on the night of that second eventful day, troops on both sides kept arriving all night and taking their places on the battlefields in the moonlight for the awful death struggle that all saw must take place the next day. And the great battle came. It was the American Waterloo. In it Lee's army, the strength, the pride, the flower of the South, went down, and with it the Southern cause. From that time on, beginning the next day with the fall of Vicksburg and the immediate appearance of the Monitor at Hampton Roads, the Southern Confederacy went downward step by step, without a single upward move, till it came to its bitter end. The fortunes of Greenbottom Inn were united with all that which the Southern Confederacy involved. On September third in the third year of the war, the opposing armies met at the Chickamauga—the river of death, and when the sun went down on that bloody battlefield, John McBride, the hero from Greenbottom Inn, lay with his face towards the sky. For him the war was over and the long night had closed in. And behind the mountains at Greenbottom Inn the sun was setting. They had on their robes of amethyst, and long shadows were in the valley. That night Celia McBride was a widow. Eunice was fatherless. The "nigger brat" also.

CHAPTER II.

Ten years! The war and its issues were gone by. The New South had set its face toward a new order of things. All the way from Mason and Dixon's line to the gulf there were wrecks of the war, and Greenbottom Inn was one of them. Celia McBride lost her husband and all her Kentucky property in the issues of the war. Ten years afterwards she had nothing left of the plantation that once belonged to the Inn but about fifty acres of cotton and meadow land. Of the Negro slaves, Aunt Rhoda, her boy, John Henry, and Daphne, the child of Lucinda, remained on the place. Aunt Rhoda was still the cook at small wages. Daphne served as housemaid but went regularly to the colored normal school at Buena Vista with John Henry. At first Celia McBride was opposed to this. She believed as most all Southerners did at first, that the Negroes had no need of education and that it did nothing but spoil them. In nearly all things Mrs. McBride's opinions were taken as law and gospel by Aunt Rhoda as completely as in slavery days, but in this one point touching John Henry, Aunt Rhoda took her freedom. In her heart she had one great ambition and that was to see John Henry a gentleman and that too after the Southern notion of a gentleman. To this end Aunt Rhoda cooked, washed, scrubbed and served "Miss Celia" with slave devotion, while John Henry went daily to school and wore good clothing. Aunt Rhoda got her reward in full measure, for John Henry grew daily into a gentleman of the truest type. He was like all boys at first. He took things as a matter of course and thought little of his mother's hard toil to give him a chance. But he wanted to learn and good habits were the natural ones for him. From the earliest childhood he was thoughtful, taciturn, and a dreamer. He was soon known as the best and most promising boy in school, at Buena Vista. He was good and obedient to his mother. Aunt Rhoda worshiped him and had every hour of toil sweetened with the thought of him, though at times for small matters she scolded him and made dire threats, none of which she ever dreamed of performing. Even with John Henry she was bound to sustain her character of severity and rebuker of sinners. And Daphne, the erstwhile "nigger brat" of Lucinda, kept her pace with John Henry. She was not particularly fond of her studies but John Henry was her master from the first and saw to it daily that she learned her lessons. Six years after the war Mrs. McBride sent Eunice to Louisville, Kentucky, to finish her education. Daphne was then twelve and had been in the school of Buena Vista four years. Mrs. McBride decided she had gone to school long enough but Daphne had her father's and Lucinda's spirit in double measure and pertly told Mrs. McBride that if she were a Negro she was a free one—that she was going to school and if she did not wish to keep her that she would go at once to the teachers' home. They had offered to take her there once before, but to this Celia McBride objected for two reasons. She hated those Northern white teachers who put Negroes on equality with them. Second, Daphne was too valuable to lose, for

27

she was smart and faithful with her house-
work if she was not too much interfered
with. Thus all objection was dropped and
for four years more Daphne trudged daily
by John Henry's side to Buena Vista and
back. It was a long walk but they were
young and thought nothing of it. Thus
the days, months, and years went by and
brought Greenbottom Inn with all its
changes ten years nearer the end of its old
life and towards the end of all things.
Aunt Rhoda however in this time seemed
not to have moved one inch in habits and
looks except to have gathered a few more
gray hairs and yielded a little more to
rheumatism. Mrs. McBride was sadder
faced and in all things another woman.
Miss Eunice had grown to the beauty of
twenty-two. John Henry was slight of
figure and looked more than his twenty
years. The "nigger brat with poison in
her blood;" now the Daphne of sixteen
years was the most changed and the most
beautiful of them all. She was too beautiful and of a beauty that can not be well
described. The jetty splendor of her hair,
the lustre of her eyes, the blending of yellow and pinkish hues of her skin, her lithe-
some and perfect form and face might have
been thought a contribution from all the

beautiful women of the ages and of all climes. Daphne was beautiful and innocent at sixteen. Her supreme gift however was that of song. She was a born musician. Her half sister Eunice was excelling in Louisville as a pianist and had also a lovely voice. Daphne had inherited her voice and deep musical instinct from her father and her mother as well, for Lucinda had been the leading singer in the palmy days of Greenbottom Inn. Eunice had full opportunity to develop all her musical talent. Daphne had almost none. But all the hills about the old Inn, the distant mountains, the ineffable beauty of springtime and summer in the valley had one and all inspired Daphne to song from the earliest childhood. She began with plantation songs and camp-meeting melodies which she first heard. But she had not been in the school long before the music teacher singled out her childish voice for its wondrous pathos and sweetness. Voice culture was not an art taught in the school, but Miss Goodwin was a true musician and she could not let Daphne's lovely voice go by without some attention. For four years she gave her lessons in singing as she had opportunity, thus at sixteen Daphne was the prima donna of that section and attracted much attention. And in all her beauty and attainments there was one watching over her and adoring her with a mighty love, though the willful, playful and joyous Daphne knew it not. Aunt Rhoda washed, ironed, scrubbed and scolded but rejoiced all the while in her John Henry, not dreaming that another had his best love. John Henry read many books, brooded often over the wrongs of the Negroes and silently loved the childish Daphne whom he commanded as no other could, but never with a word of love. Daphne was all unconscious how completely he ruled over her, for his long standing and great love for her made him at once her slave and her master. "Miss Celia" grew older and sadder. She sewed on in silence, often till far into the night for a sum of money that she had often spent for the merest trifle, with never a thought of such an hour of need to come to her. She worked hard for Eunice's sake and denied herself many comforts. Many a Southern white lady after the war, husbandless and poor, but once of wealth and ease, with the spirit of a true heroine, struggled on year after in silence and the hardest strictures of life. It was no great wonder that many of them were bitter, hated the North and the Negroes. The human heart is selfish beyond words. Many of the sufferers could not put things together and read the legitimate answers to the problems of life they were forced to work out. The most of them saw no further into things than their immediate loss of servants, carriages and the good things of this life that go along with the possession of wealth. They could only feel themselves ill-used and unjustly robbed. They could not see that they were paying the legitimate price for two hundred and fifty years of enslavement of the Negroes. Indeed, they could but feel as many feel to this day that they had only done the Negroes a favor by enslaving them. Many divines and philosophers parade the incidental civilization and consequent blessing that came to the Negroes through slavery as a cause for glorification to slaveholders and the South with unblushing conceit which could only be born of selfishness. But time modifies all things and heals all woes. Whatever bitterness of heart or philosophy of life that Celia McBride held she bravely adjusted herself to her changes. There grew a sympathy between her and Aunt Rhoda that made her lean more and more on her once slave woman, and there came a day which gave them both a cause

for rejoicing. They were both mothers,
and lived only for their children. There
came a bright Friday morning about two
weeks before Miss Eunice was coming
home after an absence of four years, when
both mothers were in the best of spirits.
Mrs. McBride forgot all else but the home-
coming of her child and listened with a
glad heart to Aunt Rhoda as she exclaimed,
"Laws, Miss Celia, I's jist dying to see dat
chile agin. I knows by dis time she's mo'n
ever de spit an' iamge of Mars John." But
for all Aunt Rhoda's talk of Miss Eunice,
it was the thought of John Henry that was
filling her heart with joy that morning.
This was his graduation day from the Colored Normal Institute in Buena Vista. The
examination of all the classes took place
in the morning, at the close of which there
was to be a grand spread, and for this
Aunt Rhoda's baskets were all filled with
good things. She was early getting her
dinner on which "Miss Celia" was to finish
so that Aunt Rhoda could get off to the
great "Turn Out." Daphne and John
Henry were already gone, but he was not
in his mother's high spirits. The riot at
Wauhallak, Mississippi, was then going
on, and there was a terrible slaughter of
Negroes. Two little boys, one white, the

other black, had met in the public road, and
the white boy, in keeping with Saxon arro-
gance the world over, demanded that the
Negro boy give the road as they met in a
place where there was mud and water with
only a narrow passage of good road. The
Negro boy refused to stand aside and a
fight ensued. The white boy got the worst
of it and went home with a bloody nose.
The father went to the Negro's cabin with
a cowhide, but the Negro father stood up
for his boy and another fight followed and
again the white brother got the worst of
it. A lynching was planned for that night,
but the Negroes got an inkling of it and
gathered secretly to defend Mose Patterson. When the lynchers approached Patterson's house the Negroes fired into them.
One white man was killed and two wounded. Terrible things followed. "An insurrection of the niggers" was announced in
the papers, with an account of the brutal
killing of an honorable white citizen of
Wauhallak and the wounding of two others, forgetting, however, to mention the
murderous intent of those honorable white
citizens who were found about midnight
on the premises of Mose Patterson. Troops
were telegraphed for and white men from
all directions poured in on the trains with

Winchester rifles. The boasted valor and bravery of the South was beautiful to see as it displayed itself against a handful of defenseless Negroes. The bloody work went on for days. The Negroes who had shown fight fled into the swamps where the white braves dared not follow, but the swamp was surrounded and the Negroes were starved out and shot down as they tried to escape. Mose Patterson was among the slain, and little James, who started the affair, was shot in cold blood. John Henry had read these reports in the papers and was almost insane from hate and silent rage. But he was cool in the examination of classes and covered himself with honor, while Aunt Rhoda sat with a beaming face listening to him. He was demonstrating a theorem in geometry when Aunt Rhoda went in, and by courtesy, as to other visitors, a book was handed to her which she held upside down. And it was just as well that way as any. What did it matter that she knew not one word of the meaning of those lines of the parallelopipedon which John Henry demonstrated with such a flow of words. She knew he was her boy, and that was enough. When he was through he waited to be questioned by the visitors, and the white board of education put question after question to him, which he answered with readiness. Aunt Rhoda, with a heart full of pride, whispered to Sister Jane Collins and said, "Jist look at dat boy ansrin' de questions whut de white folks is axin' him. He's a sho nuf gentleman!" The examination came to a close, and the great spread followed, after which Aunt Rhoda went back to the Inn in triumph, but the hour of her greatest glory was yet to come, for she was destined that night to hear her boy stir Buena Vista with a speech as it had not been stirred in many a day. When Aunt Rhoda reached her cabin John Henry was already there with the day's paper lying across his lap. It was full of the horrors that were going on at Wauhallak.

"The nigger Wade Cheatham, who has been suspected of carrying food to the niggers shut up in the swamp, was milking at sunset yesterday when eight white men rode up and told him to say his prayers if he wished. The nigger fell on his knees and begged for his life, but his prayer was answered with eight loads of buckshot!"

John Henry had stopped at this paragrah and did not seem to notice the coming of his mother. Aunt Rhoda was given to praise of John Henry behind his back but never to his face. However, on this afternoon, her heart was too full for silence.

"Chile, I's washed and scrubbed many a year to see dis day, an' I could do it as long again for yo' sake, honey."

"Mother," said John Henry, as if he had not heard a word she had said, "do you believe God loves Negroes? I don't."

She was so taken back by surprise at the question at first she could not answer, but as he kept looking at her for a reply the real Aunt Rhoda came to herself. She was one of the pillows of the church, one of the chief shouters and loudest in prayer in times of revivals and always a rebuker of sinners. John Henry might have been guilty of any offense on this afternoon without rebuke except such rank infidelity. But this was too much.

"You darsen set dar an' ax me sich a question as dat? Is dat what yo' gerometry and dictionary done brung you to? Ain't you done hearn Brer Luke preach no longer den las' Sunday at de camp-meeting how de Lawd done love dis whol' world and give His only Chile fur to save it?"

"If he loves the Negroes, mother, why does he let the white folks shoot them down all this week like dogs at Wauhallak, just as they did last fall at Durant? That Negro father had as much right to stand up for his child as that white father did for his, but that fatherly act has led to the murder of forty Negroes to one white man. Those Negroes had a perfect right to form those co-operative stores for their own benefit at Durant. That act of intelligence led to the murder of sixty-two Negroes and not to the arrest of one single white man. God may love the Negroes as he does the white people, but I don't believe it!''

Aunt Rhoda was a Negro with sympathy for her race. She had seen it abused all her life long, and there had been times when she had felt enough of what John Henry was feeling to understand him. She was silent a moment, and then replied with all her wrath gone but with a faith not to be shaken: ''Chile, I knows de Lawd lets some cur'ios things go on, but I knows he loves me 'cause I carries de witness in my breas' and I is a cullud person. Den de Bible pintly says, 'De Lawd ain't no disrespecter uv persons.' ''

''No, mother, the Bible does not say that. It says, ''He is no respecter of persons.' ''

''Well, ain't dat de same thing?'' said Aunt Rhoda, with rising wrath.

"No, mother, it is not the same thing. I think He must be a great disrespecter of some persons if He is righteous Himself."

"John Henry, you shet yo' mouf and go outen here. Put dat paper down an' go into de guarden an' hoe dem beans. De guarden is runnin' away wid weeds, an' you set here day ater day wid yo' nose stuck in dem books, which I'm gwine to burn ef you don't stir yourself mo'."

John Henry said no more. He knew his mother would burn her company feather bed before she would his books. She finished laying off her Sunday clothes, scolding all the while, and then went back to the Inn to start the supper. There she found Sister Millie White who began at once to tell her what "de white folks" were saying all over town about John Henry's fine examination. In a moment the mother-heart was too full of pride to remember his religious outbreak the hour before. By and by the sun went behind the mountain and the lights began to glimmer in the city. Soon after dark the chapel of the Normal School was packed with people eager to see and hear. An improvised stage extended all the way across the end of the chapel, and when the curtains were drawn there was a mass of all colors of faces and dress about the freshness of youth that was beautiful to see. As the young people came upon the stage from time to time there were many present who had felt all the bitterness of slavery, but who felt paid that night for all they ever bore and missed in life, so grateful were they for what had come to their children. But it was the last two exercises that took the house by storm. Daphne came out upon the stage and sang Handel's "Angels ever bright and fair." Her youth, her passionate cry and great beauty of person made her appear as an angel herself. John Henry followed with his graduating speech. His subject was "A man's a man for a' that." Burns had inspired his thought not so much as the prejudice and the wrongs of the Negroes which so occupied his thought constantly. He spoke at first what he had written for the occasion, but as he proceeded his feelings passed the flood-gates, and then for half an hour he poured out his pent up soul with such eloquence, with such fiery indignation, with such an appeal for the right and fairness and justice to all that he swept all before him. He said many a thing that was dangerous for a Negro to say, but even the whites present were so carried away with his outburst and power that the danger for the moment was small. When he closed there was the wildest confusion of yelling applause. When order was restored the certificate of graduation was given to the members of the class and the farewell song was sung and thus the school year closed. John Henry had graduated and Aunt Rhoda was glorified.

CHAPTER III.

The art exhibition in Louisville was attracting all the city. It was managed by the local art club. There were many fine collections from the best art galleries of many cities. But there was a new star appearing and his name was on all lips, partly because he was a Louisville boy and partly because his pictures on exhibition showed the touch of genius and the masterhand. He had just returned from Paris and was a young lion in society circles. His promised career was all the more romantic because he was soon to be married to Miss Eunice McBride, a young artist, prominent in musical circles. Their mothers were cousins, and the arrangement for the marriage of their children had been made before the children were old enough to know what marriage meant. But they had been taught that they were to marry each other, and they had grown up with that idea. Eunice was three years the elder. They had parted when they were at the ages of thirteen and sixteen. Joseph showed at a very early age marked talent for drawing, and at thirteen he was sent to New York where he studied four years, and then went to Paris where he studied two years, coming back to Louisville at nineteen. Thus this young couple met again and renewed the romance of their early lives. Celia McBride was now a poor woman, and there was no life fit for Eunice at Greenbottom Inn. Joseph Cramer was rich and was to return to Paris in the fall for further study. Both mothers wished the marriage to take place before he returned. One mother wished it that her daughter might be provided for as became her, and the other that her gay young son might have a stayed ballast in the gay life he was so certain to lead. Eunice was beautiful and intensely religious. Joseph was a churchman, and up to date had led an average upright life. But his very happy-go-lucky nature and the artist life which he led made him very Bohemian in his taste and habits. He was affectionate, enthusiastic,

41

emotional, generous and ready to affiliate with any sort of life which he happened to meet. The mothers were proud of their children and were happy in the thought of the coming union between them. Joseph found Eunice beautiful and ideal. He was a poet born, and music appealed to him as much as the poetry of the canvas did, and he did not altogether separate Eunice from her music, but thought himself truly in love with his promised bride. With Eunice it was different. When her beautiful cousin lover returned to her after four years, with their childhood lying behind her, her heart was still free but not in love. Joseph was beautiful. Handsome—the adjective ordinarily used for men—was not the term to use for him. His beauty was almost feminine. His hair was shining black. The lips were full, the nose straight, slightly distended at the end, making it appear large. The eyes detracted; they were of that gray which made them appear expressionless. His figure was medium and still boyish. His beauty was of that kind which goes straight to the heart of women, and it was not long till this enthusiastic and affectionate boy had won the heart of Eunice McBride. Her love was not of the ardent and demonstrative kind.

That was not her make-up, but her love was of that kind which grows and grows till lost in a life of perfect devotion. She was soon to return to Greenbottom Inn with her mother, and Joseph Cramer was to spend the summer with them. Eunice had insisted that they ought to know each other before they were married. Before they left Mrs. Cramer had decided to give a grand reception, and on the evening of the occasion, in their brilliantly lighted apartments, the two mothers, with Joseph and Eunice, received their guests with that graciousness and sociability which belong to the high-born and cultured on such occasions. Joseph was a child of favor to whom all hearts opened with fervor. He was everywhere, belonged to everybody and was idolized by all. He indulged in the flippant and light talk of the evening and he splashed and swam here and there like a fish in water. He was in almost every dance. The rudy color of youth, the excitement and happiness of the hour, was upon his face. Eunice was not jealous of him. She enjoyed his popularity. It only showed her off to better advantage as the one to be congratulated. By and by she tired of the crowds and the heat. She wandered off through the various apartments till she reached the conservatory that terminated the suite of company rooms. She passed on through palms, laurel trees and brilliant orchids till she reached a restful retreat. She sat down and indulged in beautiful dreams until she was aroused by footsteps and a gleaming face.

"Eunice, dear, I have hunted for you this half hour."

"O I don't think that can be true. I don't think you have had me in mind ten minutes at a time to-night," she said, pretending to pout.

"You know that is not a true saying," he replied, seating himself by her side. "I am having a good time to-night, Eunice, that's a fact, but you know you are the queen of my heart."

"Well, I like to see you happy, Joseph, but I could never fly around and take in so many people as you do."

"O, but life is jolly Eunice. Come, let us go in and have some more of it."

"But is not life good out here by ourselves, Joseph?"

"O, yes, but you know we are to have plenty of that every day this summer at Greenbottom Inn, to say nothing of Paris next fall and winter, but to-night, Eunice, dear, every nerve and fiber in me wants to dance. I want you to take the next waltz with me.''

And this young pair, with hope before them and life infinitely sweet at the moment, went back to the gay apartments where they were soon with the rest whirling in the maze of the waltz.

A few days later they were on the train bound for Greenbottom Inn, which place they reached about mid-night. The next morning Aunt Rhoda served a most delightful and elaborate breakfast for Miss Eunice and her cousin. She had been planning it for a week, and she was much pleased with the praise Eunice and the gay young Cramer were bestowing upon her as a cook. They chatted merrily, and Cramer was in the midst of a Paris story, over which they were all laughing, when suddenly a voice with inimitable sweetness began carolling one of Balf's songs from ''The Bohemian Girl.'' The song came from a throat as flexible as a bird's and as entrancing as a siren's. Joseph Cramer, with a face full of surprise, stopped his story and said, ''Who is that with such a voice in such a place as this?''

''Indeed,'' said Eunice, ''you are complimentary to this place, and think nothing good can come out of Nazareth, do you?''

But as he seemed to pay no attention to her reply and waited with such an eager face, Aunt Rhoda came forward with her explanation. ''Honey, 'taint nobody but dat Daphne. She's alus gwine round here singing her sinner songs. Why, when she wuz a little gal she sung speritual songs like a engil, but, bless gracious, sence dem white teachers in dat town school done got hole uv her, she don't sing nothing but dem songs with trills and runs. Why, no longer den las Cheusday I cum in here and found her wid her hans clapped togedder, her head throwed back, and singing away like she was half crying. First I thought dat she done gone clean destracted, an' I say, 'Daphne, what in de worl is de matter wid you?' Den she tucken laf, and say she was playing Magerite and Faust. When I ax her what is dat, she tole me uv a country gal in some furin lan', whar a city gent cum out to see her and spile her life, and dat de gal got rested fur pizenin' her mother, dough she didn't aim to do it. I tole her I don't want to hear no mo'er dat nonsense, and dat she better be singing some speritual songs whar gwine to be some benefit to 'er when de worl's on fire.''

This proved too much for the gravity of Joseph Cramer and he laughed till he was almost strangled. Aunt Rhoda beamed and thought he was only laughing at Daphne's folly. And all the while this Greenbottom Inn interpreter of the woe of Goethe's immortal Marguerite, through the medium of Gounod's version of it, was out by the grape arbor watering the flower beds and pouring fourth the pathos and fervor of soul as expressed by Balfe's poor Gypsy, who was losing his Gypsy lover—no longer a Gypsy but the daughter of a count from whom she was stolen in childhood and now restored to her father. With her sweet and wonderfully sympathetic voice Daphne was out by the grape arbor telling the oldest story of the world in that old and familiar song which Balfe puts into the mouth of the Gypsy—"Then You'll Remember Me." Daphne had not yet seen Eunice, and was all unconscious of her admiring audience in the dining-room. When she was through with the flowers, she went to the kitchen and came into the dining-room, supposing they were through breakfast. At the door she stopped abashed, but exclaimed, in the next impulse:

"O, Miss Eunice," the form of address she had been taught from childhood. Both

47

were surprised in what they saw in each other and that which they saw compelled mutual respect. Four years' time had done its work for both. Eunice was kind-hearted and rose to meet the kind impulse from Daphne. Joseph Cramer, the poet-painter, forgot himself completely. He arose, held out his hand and said:

"I want to know you also, Miss Daphne. I am charmed with your singing."

Eunice was shocked and Mrs. McBride was indignant beyond words. Aunt Rhoda was simply stupified. The warm-hearted and passionate Daphne saw it all. She was sensitive and proud. She drew back with fine scorn and said:

"Mr. Cramer, has your education at New York and abroad so corrupted your good manners that you, a Southern born gentleman, can insult your hostess by offering me a Negro girl, your hand and calling me Miss Daphne?"

But the impulsive Joseph Cramer was not to be stopped. Her long and wavy black hair fell luxuriantly down her back. Her face, neck and arms were perfect. Her yellow and pinkish hue of skin, heightened in richness of color by the moment of excitement, and her lovely voice and deep black eyes, made her altogether an object of beauty that went straight to the poet-painter's heart.

"I think you are wrong, Miss Daphne," he persisted in saying. "I think you are like all our colored people; you are too quick to take offense. I am a Southerner, but Southern gentlemen can recognize a lady in any race."

"Maybe so, Mr. Cramer; I am only sixteen. I have never been out of the sight of these mountains about Greenbottom Inn, but what you say is news to me. I am certain, however, that I have never come in contact with Southern gentlemen, if you are right, and I may have had the wrong opinion of them all. I beg your pardon; I have associated with one Southern gentleman. His name is John Henry, but the color of his face somewhat resembles the color of your shoes. I hardly think he is the kind you referred to, but he is a real gentleman."

Mrs. McBride swept out of the room in anger and disgust, and Eunice was much offended. Aunt Rhoda had been burning with wrath at "Dat fored Daphne" till she made her last remark, and then her feelings went completely over to Daphne's side. Joseph Cramer laughed and said:

"Well, if it offends you for me to say

Miss Daphne, I will say Daphne, especially
if that can get from you another song such
as I heard you singing before you came in
here.''

He went to the parlor where he laughingly heard Mrs. McBride's rebuke for his conduct with Daphne. Later in the morning
he and Eunice drove to the top of Monte
Sano, and there on the height of the mountain and in their love and happiness of the
hour the introduction of Daphne was forgotten. But on his way home he asked who
this John Henry was, and strange to say,
there was something in his heart akin to resentment against one he had never seen.
Was it because he resented the idea of a
Negro trying to be a gentleman, or was it
because he knew that he, whom that proud
and lovely vision he saw in the dining-room
at breakfast called a gentleman, was a gentleman. The jealousies of the human heart
are very subtle sometimes. The drive home
through the sunset mountains was so delightful Joseph Cramer was intensely happy.

''Eunice,'' he said, after one of his silent
moods, ''this is a beautiful world. I think
I would like to live in it always, that is, if
I could be young forever and have you by
my side.''

"No, not always, Joseph. I think there is a better world than this somewhere. I am happy here, and more so now than I ever was before, but this life in its very best phases is too incomplete to wish to live in it forever."

He laughed softly and said: "Let us have this one as long as we can and then the better one afterwards."

They were now come to the Inn, and Cramer was come out of his dreamy mood. As he helped Eunice from the carriage, his eyes made a swift survey of all the surrounding things for an object which he did not see.

"Well, mother," said Eunice, "we have been on the mountain top all day poetically and materially, but I am quite ready to come down to things as matter of fact as a good supper."

The mother answered the daughter only with a sigh. She had been in the valley all day. She had been thinking of the woman Lucinda.

CHAPTER IV.

Life at Greenbottom Inn became very bright with the home coming of Eunice and her cousin. Joseph Cramer brought sunshine and gay life wherever he went. The first few days at the Inn were hourly full of keen delight to him. The sight of the mountains with all the beautiful surrounding country, the flocks and herds about the Inn, and the quiet of the country life were charms beyond words to his emotional and poetic nature. He and Eunice drove out in the afternoons almost every day. She was very happy. He was also, but he kept his eyes open for a sight of Daphne, although he instinctively felt that the eyes of his aunt were upon him and for the first time in his life felt the need of retraint and artfulness in any matter that interested him. It may be that Daphne had something of the same feeling of Mrs. McBride's watchfulness, or it may have been her own modesty guided her; she at any rate kept much out of Cramer's sight at first. During the first two weeks she served in the dining-room a time or two, but as she was there as a servant no word passed between them, but they both were so conscious of each other there was left something of an impression that they had communicated with each other. Cramer was keenly sensitive to the beautiful, and this Negro girl fascinated him as no other ever had. One Saturday morning at the close of the second week at the Inn, Joseph heard Mrs. McBride tell Daphne to go to the East pasture to gather blackberries for a blackberry pie for dinner. Without a moment's thought or hesitation he went for the gun, and, meeting Eunice at the door, told her he was going to hunt awhile. He went directly west from the Inn to the Meridian turnpike, and then followed it northward till he passed the corner of the hill north of the Inn. Then he turned his face eastward along the hill towards East pasture where the blackberries grew. When he had gone about half way he sheered off to the north and went into a clump of woods north of East pasture. It was a warm morning in early June and the quiet woods invited rest and the stirring of pleasant fancies. Joseph Cramer sat down by a mulberry tree near the edge of the woods. The chirping of the birds, the hum of the insects, the gentle stirring of the leaves and the distant glimmer of East pasture were very seductive to a nature like his, and not calculated to stir him to resistance of any sort. Presently his attention was arrested by the leap of a squirrel from a larger tree into the mulberry. He raised his Winchester and fired at the little forester. It fell dead to the ground.

Cramer was a good shot, but he did not
have the spirit of the hunter, and when he
picked up the dead squirrel he felt a keen
sense of compunction for having taken its
life. He sat down and cast a look over
East pasture and immediately the thought
about the dead squirrel repeated itself in
his mind in his thought of Daphne. He
was too frank and honest to pretend to his
own mind that he had come out to hunt.
He knew that he came out for no other purpose than to pretend to happen upon Daphne as she was picking berries, but he de-
fended himself by saying, ''Heaven knows
I mean her no harm.'' That was true beyond the fact that he knew he was following an inclination in the very nature of the
case impossible, without the likelihood of
harm to come, and he could not have told
what he did mean her. Still he sat there
thinking of the girl's great beauty, her
lovely voice, and what she might be in the
world as an artist, with all her passionate
nature and artistic instincts, if she was not
proscribed by an unmerciful prejudice and
a hateful race connection, there came into
his heart a feeling of pity for her and a
sense of resentment against the mixed up
affairs of this world. In this frame of mind
he took up his gun intending to go home

the way he came, but at that very moment there came to his ears the sweetest singing and he saw in the distance the lovely Daphne coming into the pasture. She was truly a song bird and contrary to the song-bird type, she was of beautiful plumage. He watched her a long time as she moved from place to place picking berries, until the impulse to go to her mastered him. He sauntered along with his gun and dead squirrel, and was close upon her before she saw him. The blood rushed to her face and in her heart there was such a mingling of fear, embarrassment and pleasure she could not find words to answer his pleasant greeting at first. But Joseph Cramer had traveled so far and mixed with so many people of all classes he understood how to put this simple country girl at her ease. He began by talking about the fine berries, which led him into a story about a berrying excursion he made in France the summer before. It was not many minutes till his jovial spirit and frank nature together with his power to make commonplace incidents exceedingly interesting, had won Daphne into an equally free conversation. He asked her questions about her school life, praised her voice and told her what great things she could do with it if she studied.

Thus these two young people talked on, bringing their feet nearer a danger line, though there was in the heart of neither one any guile or a wish for evil. They were like bathers by the seashore. They were just outside of the ropes and did not feel the stealing in of the undertow which has dragged so many out to sea, and death. The time went by so pleasantly that Daphne did not realize that the blackberry pie for dinner was doubtful till the roar of the ten o'clock train swept around the curve at Ferns.

"O, my," she said, "it's after ten o'clock, and Aunt Rhoda will blow me sky high for being gone so long."

They started home at once, but all of Daphne's embarrassment returned. He divined its reason because the same cause for it was in his own mind. He said:

"I believe I will go by the way of the north side of the hill and perhaps I will get a shot at another squirrel."

They understood each other and from that moment there was an unexpressed but definite agreement to concealment between them. Before they parted, Joseph said:

"Daphne, I am more than anxious to hear you sing again. Will you come into the parlor and sing to-night? I will ask

Miss Eunice to invite you."

"Yes, I will come if she asks me."

Daphne was late and thought to shorten her way to the Inn by crossing some pasture land where some fine cattle were kept. Old Lycurgus, the bull, was kept in this pasture and sometimes he was vicious. Daphne did not venture in that pasture when he was at large, but she dreaded Aunt Rhoda's scolding, and with a sense of guilt in the matter of her delay, she resolved to risk crossing the pasture, as she did not see old Lycurgus about anywhere. Now it happened on that very morning all the cattle had been driven out of that pasture except old Lycurgus. He was therefore lonely and in no mood to have his domain intruded upon. Daphne was about half way across the pasture when she saw him looking straight at her. What his intentions were did not appear, but the moment he saw Daphne turn to run, his wrath burst with a mighty roar, and he started in pursuit of the fleeing girl. Daphne turned northward and ran towards the cattle shed. Joseph Cramer, who had not gone around the hill, as he said, but somewhat over it, intending to come down on the south side and after Daphne beyond the pasture, getting to the Inn after she did. He watched her crossing the pasture, saw her turn to run, and the bull in pursuit. Swift as an arrow he fled down the hill side towards the fleeing Daphne, but not in time to come between her and the mad bull. By the time Daphne had reached the cattle shed he was at her heels and she thought her last moment had come. There was an old wagon in the middle of the shed. Daphne doubled and ran on the other side of the wagon just as old Lycurgus made a deadly lunge at her. His horns crashed into the boards at the opposite end of the shed. The now thoroughly infuriated beast turned and dashed again at Daphne, who had stopped at the opposite corner of the wagon, not daring to risk a run in the opening, with the fences so far away. As old Lycurgus came at her again she darted around the wagon, but when she reached the further side she tripped and fell. It would have been but a few moments of bloody goring of the beautiful Daphne had not the bowed head with demon eyes and distended nostrils been at that moment pierced again and again with the ringing shots from the deadly Winchester in the hands of Joseph Cramer. In that moment of the peril, with the sight of Daphne at the brink of death, he saw his own heart as clear as daylight, and he held her to his breast with a passionate clasp.

"You have saved my life," she said, as she freed herself from him, and a soul of gratitude and more looked out at her eyes.

"I have saved your life, Daphne, and it is mine," he said, with such passionate earnestness that she drew away from him, and they passed on to the Inn silently.

They found Aunt Rhoda burning with wrath over Daphne's delay, and she heard the story of the adventure with but little sympathy, and as Daphne was apparently none the worse for it, she was not disposed to let her off.

"Whut in de name uv goodness wuz you doin' over dar in dat pastor medlin' long wid ole Curgus fur? An' here I is wid nothin' to make a pie fur dinner."

Whatever Mrs. McBride thought of Daphne's danger and escape, she was angry over the loss of her fine Durham bull, and notwithstanding Joseph's artless explanation of his just happening on the scene in time to rescue the girl,she had her own opinion in the matter. The whole affair put them all out of temper, and Cramer gave up the idea of having Eunice ask Daphne to sing that evening. But that night just after supper some young ladies came to call on Eunice from Buena Vista, and one of them had heard Daphne sing at the close of the school a few weeks before. She expressed a wish to hear Daphne sing, and Eunice went for her at once, and Joseph got what he wished without asking for it. Daphne brought in a large roll of her music and sang song after song, Eunice playing her accompaniments. The last two were from Schubert, "Who Is Silvia, and Where Is She?" and then she sang his immortal "Serenade." All the passion of her soul went into this song and Joseph Cramer's heart was stirred to its depths. That night, long after bedtime, he sat by his window looking out into the soft moonshine and away to the mountains wrapped in shadows and the dreaminess of the night. It was a scene peaceful enough but his heart was beating on a wild shore where there had been many a shipwreck. He sat there facing questions of life and honor that had never been brought to his soul before. He had never been given much to prayer except to repeat the form he had always said from habit, but at last when he went wearily to bed he lifted up his face to the ceiling and prayed, perhaps the first real prayer of his life. "Lord Jesus Christ, save me." That was all he said. John

Henry came home that night, and heard from Aunt Rhoda all that had been taking place in the past two weeks up to the morning episode with the bull.

"Indeed," she said, "he is as much taken wid dat Daphne as he is wid Miss Eunice an she is in de parlor singing to 'em now same as if she wuz white."

It was also a long time before John Henry slept that night. His soul was not storm tossed but it was in a desert place. Early in life "Brer Luke" had baptized him and he hal come up in the hearing of many a powerful prayer from his mother's lips. But his question to her on his graduation day revealed the doubts that ran through the mind of John Henry at times. But he was like all sceptics who have once believed. He only needed grief and anguish of soul to show him that there come times when the poor human heart has to believe whether it would or not. There come hours when philosophy and reason wont answer. Like Joseph Cramer, he at last lifted his dark face to the roof of his mother's cabin and prayed. It was Cramer's prayer over word for word with a change of pronoun. "Lord Jesus Christ save her." The next morning was Sunday and gloriously fair. About eight o'clock

John Henry went to the Greenbottom Inn Spring and saw one there he had not seen before. "Good morning, sir," he said politely but stiffly. The other said "Good morning. I presume this is John Henry."

'It is, sir, and I presume you are Joseph Cramer." In Paris this sort of an introduction would have been well enough for Cramer, but here at Greenbottom Inn and by a Negro it made his breast swell with unreasonable anger. "It is Mr. Cramer," he said with offended dignity. John Henry filled his water pail and turned away with such supreme contempt the sunny nature of Cramer burned with rage. Thus these two boys of nineteen and twenty met and parted in a moment's time with hatred in their hearts for each other. They both knew why they hated each other but neither had the remotest idea how deep was the dislike the one had for the other. Jealousy is the parent of the most bitter and the most soul poisoning of all hatred. John Henry left the Inn for Ansonia where he had begun teaching school. He had not spoken to Daphne. In the days that followed there were many calls from Buena Vista, and Eunice and Joseph were constantly returning them. But little communication passed between him and Daphne. One day he told Eunice that he was going to make a sketch of Daphne and paint her as Psyche next winter when they were in Paris. About ten days after the episode with old Lycurgus, Eunice and her mother went to Buena Vista for the day and Cramer told Daphne of his plan to paint her picture and asked her to sit for him that morning. Daphne was pleased with a child's delight with the thought of her picture being displayed in Paris. She sat patiently for Cramer an hour while he was working on the sketch. Suddenly he laid down his pencil and came over to adjust her head to a poise that he wished. He took her head between his hands and adjusted it. Then yielding to a passionate impulse he kissed the astonished Daphne twice. Shame and anger diffused her face with blood. Rising she drew back and struck Cramer in the face and left the room.

Yet beneath her anger and sense of outrage she knew in her heart there was a flame of fire for Joseph Cramer, and that by it she would be consumed unless she could get away from Greenbottom Inn. The heritage of the slave woman, Lucinda, and the dead hero of Chickamauga had come to its own. Daphne wrote to her former music teacher, telling her that she greatly desired to come North if she could get some work to do. Miss Goodwin, the teacher, thought she was better off where she was, and so wrote to advise her. If Daphne had been wise enough to have written the whole story, the reply would have been different. For a short while Daphne kept as much out of Cramer's way as she could, but in the end the almost inevitable result of the situation followed.

CHAPTER V.

The meetings between Joseph Cramer and Daphne at first apparently were by chance, but finally they met by appointment, and then the beautiful Daphne was lost. Along towards the last of August she began to loose her high spirits, and one day in the first week of September she told Cramer her condition.

"Come into the garden at eight to-night and we will talk it over," he said.

Eunice was sick all that day, and Mrs. McBride was attending to her. At six Cramer had his supper alone. There had been fitful showers of rain all the afternoon, but by supper time it had ceased to rain, though

there were still shifting clouds in the sky.
The heat had been intense for many days
and the showers of rain made the evening
delightfully cool and pleasant. After supper Cramer sat for a long time on the portico on the west of the Inn and looked at
the low mountains where there was still a
faint red tinge of sunset cloud. There was
a quietness and sweetness in the hour that
made him feel a friendship for the hills and
all the lovely inanimate life around him.
And as he watched the red clouds he whis-
tled softly an exquisite little tune, that
Eunice often sang to him at the sunset
hour, set to those beautiful words of
Moore's:

"How dear to me the hour when daylight
    dies,
  And sunbeams melt along the silent sea;
For then sweet dreams of other days
    arise,
  And memory breathes her vesper sigh to
    thee.

"And as I watch the line of light that
    plays,
  Along the smooth wave t'ward the burn-
    ing west,
I long to tread that golden path of rays,

And think 'twould lead to some bright
    isle of rest.''

This song set him thinking of Eunice,
and there came over his face a shade of tender sadness. And in this mood he sat till
the twilight had deepened into night. Suddenly he pulled out his watch and saw that
it was a little past eight. He went into the
house and into Eunice's room to inquire
how she was. It may be that the desire to
see where her mother was, took him up-
stairs as much as anything else. But in
spite of his lack of faithfulness his heart
was very tender towards Eunice and when
he saw her white face his heart filled
with pity for her. When he stooped and
kissed her a tear dropped on her face. She
smiled and said:

''I am not sick enough for a tear, Joseph, dear'' But it was not long till she
was to have much bitterness of heart softened by that tear. The silent thinking in
the twilight and the visit to Eunice put into the heart of Cramer a resolution to turn
back and try to get on the right road again,
but there was no hope for Daphne. She
understood how utterly she was lost. The
garden was damp but full of the smell of
sweet blooming flowers and the freshness

of plant life. Daphne had been in the garden some time and was weeping softly when Cramer came to her. He tried to soothe the weeping girl with avowals of love. But they had not been together long when Cyrus Bailey and his two sons, neighboring farmers who rented some cotton land from Mrs. McBride, called to see her on some business matters. They heard the loud voice of the elder Bailey say that they would not come in as it was so pleasant; they would sit out on the portico. Cramer and Daphne were too near this party for comfort.

"Let us go to the spring," he said.

They went out by a side gate and on to the spring up by the hillside. The sky was clear of clouds now and the stars were shining brightly, but there were so few people belonging to the Inn, Cramer and Daphne were but little likely to be seen together ordinarily. But there was one watching them closely whenever he was at the Inn, and he had come home that night. He went to his mother's cabin, but she was at the Inn kitchen, and by and by he went down there just in time to see Daphne go into the garden. He knew at once that she had gone there to meet Cramer, and he concealed himself to watch. He waited a long time, but by and by Cramer came out and went into the garden. His heart filled with silent rage and he was just going around to the front entrance to confront the two in the garden when Bailey and his sons rode up to the Inn gate. Not wishing to be seen by them, he went back to his hiding place and very soon afterwards Cramer and Daphne passed close by him. He followed them stealthily and came upon them at the spring. Daphne gave a stifled scream, and Cramer turned and said angrily:

"Who are you?"

"I am the one who told you that if Daphne came to any harm through you, you should pay dearly for it."

He ran upon Cramer and struck him a blow in the face that made him reel. But Cramer was not lacking in animal courage. He sprang at John Henry like an enraged lion. The two boys were about equally matched, and for a few moments it was blow for blow. Then they clinched, and John Henry got Cramer by the throat and backed him against a tree. Cramer got out his knife and tried to stab John Henry, but Daphne, who had all the while been franticly trying to separate them, prevented the knife thrust. John Henry seized the wrist of the hand with the knife and in their struggling, they came to the high rock by the spring where there was a fall of ten feet. They went over, and Cramer was under John Henry in the fall. John Henry was stunned by the fall. He soon got up but Cramer did not move. When they fell Daphne gave a piercing scream, and the three farmers, Mrs. McBride and Aunt Rhoda came running to the spring. When they came up Daphne had fled but John Henry began telling what had happened. The men took Cramer's limp form up and one of the younger said, "He is dead as sure as hell! By God, nigger, you will swing for this."

There followed terrible confusion and excitement. The neighbors were aroused and the news spread in all directions! A crowd soon gathered and there were loud threats of lynching John Henry on the spot. Aunt Rhoda ran in terror to her cabin where John Henry had already gone and told him to fly for his life. He knew too well how timely the warning was. He made his plans quickly. He took all the money they had and went out towards the mountains southeast of Greenbottom Inn. He intended to make a roundabout tour to Buena Vista and hide in the suburbs of the city till the midnight passenger train came in bound for Memphis. This was an ill-devised plan of escape, and he realized it, but he knew he must be far from Green-bottom Inn before daylight if he were to have any chance of life from the mob cer-tain to be on his track with bloodhounds in a few hours. Near the depot there was an old unoccupied building in which he hoped to hide until the train began to pull out, and then he would run and jump on it. He knew the danger in trying to escape in this way, but he thought it less risky than taking to the woods. The two Bailey young men rode in haste from the Inn to Buena Vista with the news and in a little more than an hour's time a mob was on its way to Greenbottom Inn. When it found that John Henry had escaped,the mob went back to Buena Vista and a systematic hunting party was organized. Blood-hounds were taken to the Inn and all the streets leading into the city were guarded, but soon after 11 o'clock John Henry got safely into the city, being too wise of the probable movements to enter by any of the streets but by cross lots and alleys. When the mob reached the Inn the second time they had the dogs with them and went at once to Aunt Rhoda's cabin. The old

mother was wild with grief and begged
that wild, heartless mob to spare her child
and insisted that it was only an accident.
But one of the company cursed her roughly and asked her if that speech he made at
the exhibition in May was an accident. He
told her, "He was too damned smart, but
he would soon be where all smart niggers
belonged." The dogs were put on John
Henry's trail, and when Aunt Rhoda heard
their dreadful baying her heart sank within her. She fell on her knees and wrestled
all night long as did Jacob of old. "O,
Lawd, save John Henry frum de mob."
That was the bitter cry that went out into
the night from her anguished stricken soul.

When John Henry started for Buena
Vista he went southeast from the Inn till
he crossed Moore's creek. He then went
forward a half mile and then came back as
nearly in his tracks as he could. Then he
entered the creek which was shallow at
this season and waded down it for two
miles, coming out just opposite Buena
Vista. In this way the hounds were baffled and he was not traced to the city. In
the meantime the crowds grew and the
mob spirit proportionately. A large crowd
was assembled on the public square, and
one known for cruel deeds among the Ne-

groes made a fiery speech against the whole race. He paraded the fact that this here John Henry had been ruined by them Northern white folks who had come down here to lead the "niggers" out of their place, and this here John Henry on the night of the "nigger turn-out" had tried to rouse the "niggers" to insurrection, and he did not see why the honorable white citizens let him pass then. But they did, and what the result—a white young man—a white young man who was among them as a visitor, a young man of renown, this night lay dead, foully murdered by this upstart of a "nigger." What will you do with him?

"Lynch him! Lynch him!" came from five hundred or more throats.

The mid-night passenger train at last came steaming into the city. From his hiding place John Henry could see that the crowd at the depot was on the lookout for him. He dared not come out, but as the train began to ring its bell for moving on he grew desperate and as the train began to move he started from his hiding place. But he was seen as soon as he emerged from the old building. The cry was given and a crowd of men and boys made a rush for him with a loud shout. He turned by the old building in which he had been hiding and ran down a dark alley with the yelling crowd coming on behind. He leaped the fence in the dark and doubled in the railroad yard and came out just above the depot, while his pursuers went on down the alley. He crossed the railway track and ran into a by-street leading towards the southeastern portion of the city. He hoped to gain Moore's creek at the nearest point by going in this direction, intending to wade down it again for a distance and then make for the mountains. But he had not gone far till he ran into two policemen. One of them knew him well and liked him. John Henry saw that it was all up and did not try to make further escape. He told Mr. Riley how it all was, and begged him to get him in the jail secretly, which he did, but it was soon noised abroad that he was captured and was in jail. The mob howled with glee, and in a little time a thousand men, boys and women were in front of the jail. They demanded John Henry at once. The jailer made some show of resistance, but he was soon overpowered and the keys were put into the hands of the leader of the mob. In his cell John Henry heard the lynchers at the door of the jail and he knew that his life was lost. At first he was in great terror at the thought of the dreadful torture and death which he knew was in store for him at the hands of those demons outside. He thought of his old mother and Daphne and his heart almost broke with anguish. Then there came to him that wonderful will-power and self-command which he had always had. And in this last hour he lifted up his grief-stricken face and prayed: "Lord I don't understand Thee, nor Thy ruling of this world, but I resign myself into Thy hands. Do what you wish with me. I ask Thee to forgive all sinful thoughts of rebellion which I have ever had. Take care of my old mother and Daphne. Forgive my soul of all sin. Amen!"

Then he waited for the coming of the mob and he did not have to wait long. Cruel and merciless hands dragged him from his cell and from the jail steps he saw a sea of faces. And there were devils incarnate there. See once a mob lynching a Negro with all the hate and cruelty of the heart let loose, and there can be no doubt of a personal devil and how supremely he gets possession of many hearts. When John Henry appeared there was a wild rush for him, but the leader of the mob beat the

zealous back. It was the speech-maker
earlier in the evening on the public square.
He could not let the opportunity pass for
another display of his eloquence and gen-
eralship in the matter of lynching niggers.
He proceeded to address the crowd again
with the same speech he had delivered already, and when he referred again
to John Henry's speech at the "nigger turn-out" in May, some one in the
crowd suggested that, perhaps, the "nigger" would like to make a speech to-night.
The leader thought it a good joke and
asked John Henry for an address.

He stepped forward and began with a
coolness that so amazed them all there was
immediately an intense hush. He said: "I
thank you for this last chance to address
you. I was born here and all who know
me know that my conduct from childhood
has been blameless. I did fight Joseph
Cramer to-night and in the struggle we
fell and he was killed by accident. I am
no murderer. I did speak against lynching last May, and I do so again to-night.
I said then no brave and true man ever
helped to lynch a man; only cowards and
cut-throats did. I say the same to-night.
That is what you are, every one of you!"

A yell of rage as if from a thousand devils rent the air. The rush for the "audacious nigger" could not be resisted. In the scramble that followed his clothing was nearly torn off of him, and he would have been killed outright had not the leader of the mob been determined that the lynching and torture should take place in due order. John Henry was pulled away from the mob and pushed inside the jail door till the fury of the mob was abated somewhat. Then the poor, half-conscious boy was dragged through the streets almost naked, bleeding and torn towards a bridge that spanned Moore's creek where the torture and death common to savages was to be outrivaled by the high civilization of the white South.

CHAPTER VI.

It was Sunday morning. The three mountains looked up from the South in solemn silence. All the glamor of the late summer was still glorious on the mountain sides and in the valley below. The Jessamine far from its native Persian and Arabian home, filled the air about Greenbottom Inn with a subtle sweetness and vague suggestion of Oriental life. There was fallen a silence on the old mansion, such as reigns only in the presence of the king of all men, and he was came to the Inn that morning. In the parlor Joseph Cramer lay before him in state. He was wrapped about in white garments. The immaculate sheets of linen were turned back from his breast, making his crown of black hair and the dress suit of clothes more sable by contrast. He wore white gloves, and the right hand resting on his breast held a white rose. He was dressed as the bridegroom he had expected so soon to be. His full and sensuous lips were still faintly red with the look of life. They were slightly parted and the expression of his beautifully curved mouth was that of pleased wonder—that which was accustomed to be seen when he was looking upon a beautiful picture for the first time and all the passion of his soul was stirred. He was more beautiful in death than in life. There was then a beauty of form and face from which all passion and the lust of life had gone out, leaving behind only an expression of innocence and meek submission. Thus Joseph Cramer, the poet painter, slept in the Sunday morning silence of Greenbottom Inn.

*   *   *   *   *   *

On that same Sunday morning there was

another picture more marvelous to see and once seen never to be forgotten. Monte Sano was majestic still with a dignity it never lost. Towards the west it broke off with a cliff-like descent. At its feet lay Buena Vista. Far westward were the lowlands and the immediate depression of the Tennessee, which with its yellow waters sweeps down in a loop into Northern Alabama and then back into its native state. From the brow of Monte Sano it was a yellow thread slipping by the grain fields and meadow lands in the distance. The sight from the mountain's brow must have been something like the well watered plains of the Jordan upon which the covetous Lot lifted his eyes and made choice, leaving his uncle Abraham the mountains that there might be peace among the herdsman. And Monte Sano had the peace of the mountains in that Sunday morning air. Fragrant with the breath of the vintage, the soft breezes of early September swept down the mountain side, gently stirring the leaves of the trees, and far down in the valley the blades of the green corn.

But just outside of the city where the base of the mountain begins to be there was a great multitude which spoke not of peace and the Sabbath rest. There were gathered there all classes and conditions of men. There were those who looked on in silence at a sight terrible to see. There were some who jested and laughed and others who were loud with curses on the whole Negro race. There was a bridge spanning Moore's creek and over this a sycamore stretched out a white arm. There was a rope of hemp attached to this and a Negro boy at the other end. There was no black cap to hide the face, and the sight of the death agony. The eyes were starting from the socket and the tongue protruded from the mouth. Agony and despair, supreme torture was the story of the face. Nearly all the clothing was torn from the body. There was a gaping knife wound in the shoulder. The bullet holes were possible suggestions of mercy. Down the right leg there was a long seam of blood, and on the flooring of the bridge there was a dark blot for a silent testimony. The Sunday morning breeze came down from the mountains and swayed the body to and fro. It was the only thing that had touched it gently. And this ghastly work of destruction, that was once John Henry, who wore store clothes and was Aunt Rhoda's gentleman, swaying in the Sunday morning breeze, turned first one side and then the other that all might read the signs he bore. Chief above all the wounds there were these two signs for all to read. On the breast pinned to what shirt remained, in large print—"Death to him who takes him down before the sunrise tomorrow!" On the back, "Done by five hundred of Alabama's best citizens."

* * * * * *

And when the Sunday night came on there was a third picture to see, but with shadows so dark only the outlines were apparent. There was an old woman who sat all nigh in the darkness of her cabin. She was said to be powerful in prayer. She did not pray that night. Her lips had lost that form of speech. There was not much pain either, for body and mind had almost lost that capacity. There was just a dull stupor with flitting moments of memory and anguish. Once the mind went backwards twenty years and those old lips murmured soft and sweet words to a little fluffy bundle of new life. Later, in the darkness there was heard a low laughter and a chuckle, "Jist look at datt boy anserin' de question whut de white folks ax him." A clatter of horse feet by some belated rider passing her cabin swept away the vision of the examination scene and brought back the clatter of the riders the night before. A wild cry of agony which had gone out all night before in prayer passed the lips again—"O Lawd, save John Henry from the mob." Out into the pitiless night went this bitter cry again and again till exhaustion and blessed oblivion came once more. Then all was still. A little mouse came out of its hole with shining eyes and looked awhile at the prostrate form and then darted away to its hiding place. By and by the moon came up over the mountains and sent a shaft of light into the cabin making more silvery an old head already white with the toil of slavery and the sorrows of many years. The mid-night passenger train on the Memphis & Charleston road came past Mercury with a shriek, leaving behind it a trail of sparks and smoke. It turned the curve at Ferns and began ringing the bell for Buena Vista, where it stopped for a moment. But the engine was heard to roar on as if impatient for the race onward. With a mighty snort the great iron steed sped on and on to its terminus, bearing its freight of human life, bending, leaning and twisted in all positions asleep. The roar of the train became fainter and fainter till there remained only the silence of the night. But all things come to an end at last. The gray dawn stole into the cabin—that gray dawn which is the most ghostly of all the night. The old woman felt its chill, that chill of the dawn which is like death—like death because it is the forerunner of the day, as death is. All at once the old woman's senses became alert, and she thought she was coming out of a bad dream. There came into her soul a great longing to pray and she lifted up her stricken face, but before she could open her lips she heard John Henry's question again, "Mother, do you believe that God loves colored folks? I don't." There was a stifled cry like that of a lost soul. "O John Henry! O, my John Henry!" That was all of her prayer. Aunt Rhoda, powerful in prayer, the chief shouter in revivals and a rebuker of sinners at all times, was in the dark. She had lifted up her face to pray to her God, but he was gone from his throne. He was swaying to the breeze with hemp and death in the gray dawn over the bridge of Moore's creek.

*　　　*　　　*　　　*　　　*　　　*

The carnival of flowers and the festival of light and redemption had come. It was the glorious celebration of the day of the resurrection. The green grass and the tender leaves were prophecies of new life and a yearly repetition of the blessed promise that the dead shall live again. Six maidens, with young hearts full of hope for all the blessed conditions of life, were clad in white and veiled as young brides. They were making their way daintily along to the "Church of our Merciful Saviour," where they were to be confirmed at the Easter service.

While the worshipers came flocking into the church the organ was sending out sweet strains of music full of the sound of triumph. At the altar there was a bank of flowers and above them those memorable words from that tomb belonging to the rich man of Arimathaea—"He is not here: He is arisen." Hearts thrilled with joy as they read anew that wondrous announcement and many, as they came in knelt at their seats in silent prayer. It was an hour of holy communion in which hearts for the time at least were lifted above the baser things of life, and at the close of the service there was a thrill of ecstacy in all hearts when a voice of wondrous grace and sweetness poured out that song of songs from Handell's Messiah, "I know that my Redeemer liveth." And at that same hour, not far from the bridge where John Henry had swayed to the breeze in death there was another promise of new life hidden away from the sight of the world. At the base of the mountain there was an old cabin in which dwelt an aged couple who had not put of mortality for immortality of the resurrection day. But in them immortal life had long begun to be. They were royalists, having kinship with Him "who was conceived by the Holy Ghost, born of the Virgin Mary, suffered under Pontius Pilate, was crucified, dead and buried; descended into hell and the third day arose from the dead." They had kinship with that man, for one day in the fall before this blessed Easter they had seen him sitting on a stone at the base of the mountain, homeless and an outcast from the world. He was weeping, and they dried His tears with tender words of compassion and took Him in. And He told them again that on the morning of the great resurrection that they should have new life that should be everlasting. They did not go to church on this glad day, but they were His very own. In one corner of their cabin in bed there was a young face which might have served Corregio for one of his pale Magdalenes. The

wealth of black hair hanging loose about
her neck and shoulders in its careless freedom did but heighten the beauty of her
face. The hour of woman's supreme agony had come and gone for her the day before. The young mother lay all through
the glorious Easter morning in a dreamy
sweetness of half sleep and the restful
sense of deliverance. By her side there
was now and then a faint cooing and gur-
gle of new life. To these inarticulate
sounds the pale face, half child and half
woman, turned with such unutterable tenderness and ineffable love it could not seem
that such a sweet maternity and such a
little bit of holy life could be the fruit of
sin that it was. Old Aunt Jemima was
busy about her dinner when she heard a
startled cry and pitiful moan that hastened
her to the bedside of mother and child.
The old woman comforted the weeping
mother and child with tender words and
told her husband in the shed kitchen where
the dinner was cooking: ''I believe dat po'
thing in dar is gwine 'stracted.'' And
such she could but believe for she could
not understand what she saw when the
mother's cry brought her to her bed to
see her clutching the little child's hands
with such wild words about it. The little

babe had sucked its finger till the blood
was drawn to the finger tip, making it
blood red and then held it up as if for the
mother to see. In that hour of weakness
and confused senses, by some law of memory, the young mother was the little Daphne again. With a look of pain and terror
she showed Aunt Jemima the baby's crimson finger, and repeated the words that
had passed her own baby lips long before,
"She's a nigger brat with poison in her
blood."

*　　*　　*　　*　　*　　*

The time came when Celia McBride lost
all worldly possessions and she and her
daughter were numbered with that class
designated by the Negroes of the South as
"pore white trash." Greenbottom Inn
was put up for sale. The colored normal
school outgrew its city bounds. The Northern white teachers were replaced by colored teachers. An energetic young Negro
known in that community as Professor began to look for wider territory for the
school, of which he was made principal.
The industrial features of the school were
made prominent in it by him. Old Greenbottom Inn was finally bought for this
growing colored school, and thus it came
about that this once famous Inn, which

in times past entertained Negro traders, passed for an inheritance to the Negroes, where there is now new life and new hope in the new order of things, while Greenbottom Inn, as it was, is only a memory.

FOR ANNISON'S SAKE.

Love is a flame that burns with a sacred
    fire,
And fills the being up with sweet desire;
Yet, once the altar feels love's fiery breath,
The heart must be a crucible till death.

Say love is life; and say it not amiss,
That love is but a synonym for bliss.
Say what you will of love—in what refrain,
But knows the heart, 'tis but a word for
    pain.

Two abreast from Turner and Langston
Halls the girls in sections quietly marched
to the chapel. But the boys, under the of-
ficers in charge, from Sea Hall and the Annex, with soldierly bearing came to Chapel
to the martial strains of the school band.
This manner of coming to the Sunday
morning service grated on the feelings of
the chaplain and seemed out of the fitness
of things at first. But in time he got used
to it and on the last Sunday morning in
May—Commencement Sunday, the march-
ing tramp of the students and the gay air
of the band hardly arrested his attention,

so intent was he on the thought of the hour
and so great was his anxiety over his sermon. He had spent much time and prayer
over it. It was the last one he would
preach to the graduating class. He had
just been one year in the school, and only
one year out of the Theological Seminary.
He had come to his work with much zeal
but he knew that he had not made much
religious impression on the students and
especially on the graduating class. On this
morning he felt that he must reach the
class with a telling message. It was his
last chance. His very anxiety and intense
desire had made the preparation of the sermon more difficult than usual and much
more unsatisfactory when it was done. At
the beginning of the week he had chosen for
his text the passage found in the sixteenth
chapter of Matthew, eighteenth verse:
"And I say also unto thee, That thou art
Peter; and upon this rock I will build my
church; and the gates of hell shall not pre-
vail against it." "The church of Christ,"
was the subject of the sermon. He meant
to discuss it as "Visible and Invisible" in
the whole scope of its significance and con-
clude his discourse by urging them to use
their power and education for a more complete establishment of His organized

Church in the communities where their lots
would be cast. First he took down a book
from his library on difficult passages,
knowing that the text he had chosen and
those connected with it were among the
most difficult of difficult passages, for on
them and the whole structure of the bishop-
ric of the Romanist and all Churchmen are
established and exalted and from which a
large part of protestant churches dissent.
He went carefully over some seminary
notes and then read the chosen passage
from Tischendorf's Greek text, noting
carefully the readings according to Alpha,
Beza and others of authority. Suddenly he
was seized with an almost uncontrollable
laughter. In the midst of his careful
weighing of debatable points by the greatest scholars of the ages the thought of the
class, for whom he was making preparation intruded itself. Near the close of the
term they had done six weeks of required
Bible study with him and on one occasion
reference to the Ten Commandments came
up and not one in the class had any idea in
what part of the Bible they were to be
found and he knew from the knowledge
the study had displayed if he should quote
half of the books of the Old Testament for
the New not half the class would know the

difference. "No," he said to himself, "I will not do it. I will just put all this aside. I will talk to them about salvation and the abiding love of Jesus Christ. I will let that be my parting words with them." He then turned to Matthew twenty-seventh and forty-second: "He saves others, himself he cannot save." "Yes, I will take that, Christ on the cross is the supreme expression of love." And so through the week the cross and redeeming love were in all his thoughts and preparation.

Sunday morning was glorious. The crowds came as only crowds come in Northern Alabama about Buena Vista to the commencement of the Industrial and Normal school. When the Chaplain came in the Auditorium was crowded. The usual liturgical exercises were gone through and then came the sermon. He was evidently nervous and found it hard to get well started. He preached without manuscript. Again and again he was interrupted by late comers whom it was difficult to seat in the already overcrowded space. A baby irritated by the heat and crowding began to cry. The frantic efforts of the mother to quiet it only made it worse and turned the whole attention of the audience upon her and the child. The confusion of the moment and evident inattention of the class made him desperate and he began to flounder miserably in his sermon. Finally the mother took the crying child out and the audience at once fell back from its diversion but it is not likely that it would have turned very intently upon the sermon but for an unexpected turn. The Chaplain immediately ceased speaking and a most agonized face was lifted upward. They thought he had forgotten his sermon. The heart breaking prayer for help was not put into words, so those looking intently upon him now did not know. In a moment he seemed to come to himself and the power of assurance that came to his heart they all felt through his words and he began as if there had been no break. "He saves others, Himself He cannot save." "Yes, that was just it young friends. Unwittingly that band of Jews with their hearts full of unspeakable malice, in their very hour of triumph and words of reviling uttered but the truth which He had been declaring of himself. This old world was sinking down! down! down! and this man I am talking to you about came to save it." "It was love my friends that brought Him down to us." Thus on and on he went full of passionate appeal. His heart was full

of tenderness and yearning for these young
people and they were now following him
with rapt attention. He closed his appeal
by urging them to follow after the best
things of life. He pointed out to them the
great temptations they would have in the
eagerness of their laudible attempt to get
ahead in life and to use their education to
bear down the weaker rather than to bear
them up. He dwelt on the great love of
Christ for the world and how that love is
conquering men in every land. ''My young
friends let me say as a last word to you
that there is nothing equal to it in power.
Nothing like it. The love of parents for
their children is most God-like but such
love can not be separated from poor human
folly and pride. The love of the lover for
the lover may be sublime, and often is, in
all its manifold bearings on life and capacity for devotion and sacrifice, but the no-
blest of such love can never wholly be free
from passion and selfishness. But O! the
love of Christ for mankind is sublime and
free from all possible connection with
sin.'' And in this strain of almost over-
wrought tension the sermon came to its
end and the crowd as if suddenly freed
from some great power that for the time
fastened down upon them beyond their

own will, began to move, laugh and talk as such a crowd will.

Now it happened, as it often does, that efforts we put forth with all our heart fail to reach those for whom they were intended, but bless others whom we had not thought of. Although the seniors had finally given close attention and some response of heart, in ten minutes after the benediction was pronounced they dismissed the chaplain and his sermon, for the time at least, wholly from their minds. But there was one in the audience who had drunk in every word the chaplain had said, and her heart had thrilled with emotion and love all the time he was speaking, though she had been no where in his thoughts and efforts. Annette Summers had come down from the mountain for one year of schooling and it had been a glorious year for her. "O, I love like that," she had whispered to herself. "Yes, I would die for Annison. 'And greater love hath no man than that,' he said while he was preaching. I could die for Annison I know. And because God has been so good to me I will serve him all my life. I will organize a Sunday School as soon as I get home. I haven't got much voice to sing but I will teach all these pretty songs to Annison and he can lead

them. He will do fine for that." "O! Annison, God only knows how I love you."
So Annette went from the sermon glorified
in the ardor of her love for Christ and for
Annison, never dreaming that there might
be any inconsistency in linking the two together. That night this same mountain
girl sat by her window gazing with inex-
pressible tenderness out into the glorious
moonlight as it fell down in all that lonely
valley towards Buena Vista. The cries of
a thousand night things were in the air.
The perfume of the honeysuckle and the
subtle sweetness of the jessamine came up
to her, bringing messages of love and the
tenderest memories of a certain little valley
lying off in the mountains. The moon rose
higher and higher up over Monta Sano,
and the low mountains round about
bleaching them into gray mysteries and in
their onward stretch melting them away
into vague immensities. But mightier than
all and above all was the love in Annette's
heart for Annison. Early the next morning she was awakened from her love
dreams by a message that brought an anguish to her soul that could only be measured by the depths of her great love.

That same bit of yellow paper which has
brought heart-break to so many, read:

"Come home. Annison is dying." Late
that afternoon they met her at a little way
station in the mountains and these were the
first words that greeted her: "Annison is
conjured."

That was the story which had gone from
cabin to cabin all through the valley. For
three days Annison had lain in a strange
stupor, speechless and knowing no one.
Next day after Annette came home a bird
at sunset flew into the room where Annison
lay and fluttered about in terror until it
found its way out. Early in the night old
Bull, Annison's dog, came to the door and
howled three times. Then Annette knew
Annison was doomed. These were two sure
signs of death. Out in the darkness and
down the lonesome pathway of Lunny's
Hollow, Annette, with unspeakable anguish, sped on and on to old Martha's cabin. Martha knew she would come that
night. She was the arch-princess of "conjurers" among the negroes of the hollow.
Martha was ignorant, but a keen reader
of human nature and a shrewd old woman.
That mysterious power, given a few, by
which they can sway the faith and souls of
others, was old Martha's in a marked degree.

The gift, false in all its claims, but nevertheless powerful and believed in by the ignorant of all nations, had traveled down through the ages from her ancestral Africa, and rather indeed farther back than that, from the families of Asia, to make the old woman in Lunny's Hollow looked up to and feared by the negroes and many of the whites. Martha went with Annette to see Annison as soon as Annette got home and she saw what Annette's eyes blinded with love and hope did not see. Old Martha lived by her art and never risked her reputation incautiously. Her only pledge to Annette was that she would consult her "kards and coffee-grounds" the next day to see who had "tricked Annison" and to find out the nature of the spell he was under. So that night when Annette, with a face of woe, burst in upon her, old Martha was ready for her. "O, Aunt Martha, a bird flew in the house at sunset and to-night old Bull howled three times before the door! Save Annison, Aunt Martha. O! Lord, Lord, save him." "I knowed all dat befo you cumed, Annette." Old Martha's adopted daughter, Matilda Ann, was in the room, but she paid no attention to Annette. She had not spoken to her for a long time. She said Annette was "Stuck up, kase she wuz yaller;" and once Annette

98

remarked laughingly: "Eph Divens was as ugly as ho-made sin." Eph was Matilda Ann's adored. "Annette," said old Martha, "how much does you love Annison, and what would you do to save him?" There was something so playful in her tone Annette's heart gave a mighty bound of hope. "How much does I love Annison? How much would the world weigh if it was all gold? How much is the love which all the women of these valleys and mountains has for their husbands and lovers? That is how much I loves Annison, and what would I do to save him? I would crawl to the end of the world on my knees, and die after I got there if that much more was needed to save him." "Would you Annette," in a tone bordering on derision. There was a gleam of contempt in her eyes, and a sort of malicious pleasure which she would take in seeing Annette quail before the ordeal which she had in store for her. Old Martha had had the homage of fear and veneration for her power, but love, never. She was not mean at heart, but she was human, and had missed that something which softens all hearts and gives old age tender memories to cling to. For the lack of it there had come into her heart a bitterness which she hardly knew existed and the exact nature of which she could not have explained beyond that feeling of resentment which Annette had aroused by her passionate avowal.

''Well, I will tell you what will take Annison fum onder his spell and save him. Here is four bags. If you takes 'em to Sunset Rock on Shagg's Point and throws 'em, one to de east, one to de no'th, one to de west, and one south, 'zactly at midnight, and says what I tells you, 'zactly at midnight, mind you, you and Annison will live together.''

Annette gave a stifled scream of horror. Shagg's Point to the negroes of Lunny's Hollow was the abode of all evil spirits in the hobgoblin world. For his life's sake no negro would venture there alone at night. Martha knew this all too well, and then it was five miles from her cabin to Sunset Rock, and it was then half past nine. She would have been glad to have given Annette an easier task, but her reputation was at stake and the task must be an impossible one. A bold and strong mountaineer would have found nothing impossible in this task with two hours and a half of time, but old Martha knew that Annette, weak and terrified, could not make the trip in time if she dared—that is,

Martha thought she knew that, and ran no risk by imposing the task. But there was something in Annette's heart that old Martha had never known; a something that had made many a maiden weaker than Annette perform greater feats than this one imposed by old Martha. She underrated the power of Annette's love. At first she did falter and say, "O! My Lord, Aunt Martha; ain't there some other way?" "No dere ain't, and dat's a heap easier en crawling to de end uv de worl on yo' knees."

Matilda Ann had looked on in silence, but there is one sorrow that will move the hearts of all women into sympathy with one another. Matilda Ann had been bitter towards Annette, but there was a secret sadness in her own heart which pleaded for Annette.

Annette had a little education and a gift of speech which poor Matilda Ann did not have. She was greatly moved by Annette's avowal of her love for Annison. At that moment somewhere away down the Mississippi was her own Eph, who might be sick unto death, and she as Annette some day. She could not have expressed her love with Annette's eloquence, but she knew that in her heart that love was all there—that love which her slow tongue and thick lips could never truly utter, but she knew it was all there for Eph as in Annette's heart for Annison. How much she was moved was summed up in her brief statement: "I will go long wid Annette, Mammy." Only those who can understand her deep superstitions and full belief in all the repeated terrors of Shagg's Point can fully appreciate Matilda Ann's offer.

"No, Annette must go by herself or Annison dies this night."

"Give me the bags, then, Aunt Martha," said Annette, with sudden force born of love and despair. At the door she turned with all the anguish of a lost soul, and said: "Aunt Martha, if I don't get back, tell Annison how I went there to save him." For a moment old Martha's heart softened, and she was tempted to call Annette back and tell her the truth. Then she muttered to herself: "I'se got to live; it won't do. Den dere ain't nothin' up dar to hurt her. Let her go 'long." Annette went out into the night and on and on in the dark. It was June. A shower of rain had fallen early in the evening, and still there were shifting clouds in the sky. There was a sweet smell from the damp earth and the green woods. The wild flowers were hidden in the darkness, but they sent out a sweet and silent greeting to Annette. One by one the clouds were withdrawn and the sheets of mist about Shagg's Point glided away. The moon was peeping up over the head of the mountain and Sunset Rock clearly defined against the molten sky jutted out as a personification of majestic solitude.

Suddenly Annette felt a cold chill pass over her. As she looked at Shagg's Point, for a moment she saw stand out against the background of yellow sky, something— a mere speck it was, yet in shape like that of a man, which passed Sunset Rock to a shadow beyond. She thought it was an evil spirit, and she knew she was going to her death, if she went on to Shagg's Point. For a moment her courage forsook her. "O, my Lord, won't you save Annison without my going up there," she cried in her anguish. Some where from out of the air—there on that lonely mountain road, she heard it, as plainly spoken, as she did when the Chaplain said it the Sunday before: "He saves others; Himself he cannot save." She understood now. "I said I could die for Annison," she murmured to herself. Resigned now and determined, once more she set her face towards Shagg's Point; on and on she sped, climbing, stumbling, and often falling, but always on. "Annison," she kept murmuring, as if in a last good-bye. At last a few minutes before midnight, she reached the crown of Shagg's Point. There before her, Sunset Rock, with the moonbeams sweetly asleep upon it, lay stretched out, a mighty cliff over a frightful abyss. The scene was so peaceful Annette approached half in hope that the evil spirits were all present. How far away sometimes are the evils for which we look, and how near those which we do not suspect. Out from the copse near Sunset Rock, two keen and merciless eyes were watching Annette as she approached. At first there was amazement and fear, but soon there was a gleam of gloating triumph. Bill Hoard, the notorious murderer and outlaw of the mountains, knew Annette of the valley. He knew old Martha and Annison. He knew the superstitions of the Negroes and all their terrors of Shagg's Point. He did not know of Annison's sickness, but he knew some terrible and desperate measure forced Annette to Shagg's Point at midnight. "Ah, ha, my fine lady; conjuration, is it? When I asked you to come and live with me you called me a thief and the low down scrapings of poor white trash. When

I told you any sort of a white man was good enough for a nigger, you spit in my face and got slapped down. And now you have come all the way to Shagg's Point to hunt Billy up. The Giant's cave is not as good as the cabin I invited you to, but you won't mind that, my fine lady.'' Poor Annette! And this reward for high and exalted love? No; unseen in the soft moonlight, the most compassionate pity was walking by Annette's side. Out upon the broad platform of Sunset Rock she stepped. Her fear was almost gone. On the east, north and west there was a ledge of rock over which one might step to an abyss of two thousand feet below. To the south only was there a retreat from Sunset Rock. Annette turned first to the east, where the sky was golden with gleams and murmured her charm, and then threw her first bag. With the throw to the north went a mighty wave of love, for there far down in the dark shadows of the valley was Annison, whom she was saving. Then to the west she repeated her charm. Now half gleeful, all fear for the moment gone, she turned to the south to complete her work of magic. The incantation died on her lips. Horror palsied the uplifted hand. There in the dreamy moonlight, with a tiger's tread, sure of his victim, was a man approaching, who to Annette's dilated vision was the father of giants and evil spirits. There was one moment of silent agony, and then with a scream that went up to the stars, Annette was over Sunset Rock. Next morning, June was glorious with its soft blue sky and meadows of green grass in the valley. On Shagg's Point the hemlock boughs gracefully nodded to the cool breezes which swept down the sides of the mountain to the valley below, carrying with them sweet breath of new life. Racing up and down an old chestnut, two gray squirrels were chattering and playing like a newly married pair. The trees were full of birds, which filled the air with chirping and singing, where the leaves were trembling and shaking out silvery glitters and dancing shadows to the ground.

Under Sunset Rock, more than a thousand feet below, on a shelf of the mountain side, there was a little patch of broken stones and heap of earth, which doubtless had fallen in some little avalanche from the brow of the mountain long ago. Growing out from the stones and earth were some mountain laurels. There was a little stream of water that trickled from a cleft in the rock wall. Here in a niche was the home of a family of wrens which had dwelt there for generations undisturbed in all their bliss of bird life.

By the side of that short stream, down to the very edge where it leaped to the depths below, the wild lobelia flamed in crimson glory. Wherever there was earth enough for their tiny roots, the violets were rioting in gay profusion. Entangled with laurels a winding grapevine formed a hammock of living green. Half hidden in green leaves of that tangled vine was an object lodged high on the mountain side, and over it there was a great chattering and confusion among the wrens. Attracted by this, a searching party, by means of rope ladders, found the object of its search— bruised and unconscious, but alive.

The reputation of old Martha, the princess of conjurers, was maintained, for her word had come true. "Mind you," she had said, "ef you is dar zackly at midnight Annison will git well." Almost an hour after Annette had stood on Sunset Rock, just as the hand of the clock pointed ten minutes to one, Annison suddenly seemed conscious. He raised himself up on his elbow in bed, and with a smile said: "Annette, how beautiful you looks." He then lay down again and went to sleep. The next morning when the doctor came in he stopped near the bed in amazement and exclaimed: "Why, Annison, a miracle must have taken place last night!"

There had indeed, for, away up the mountain side, under Sunset Rock, LOVE had conquered Death.

A CREOLE FROM LOUISIANA.

In the new sunshine of the early morning, Lizzie Story used to pass by Green-bottom Inn, and go out towards Mercury, on the old slave track, leading into Northern Alabama from North Carolina and East Tennessee. But that was soon after the late Civil War, and Lizzie Story was free—free born. She was far from her native home at Watch Hill, Rhode Island, where you behold the sea stretching away into an immeasureable waste that makes you think of Eternity, and where you can see the white ships sailing away until they go out of sight at that point where the sea and the sky come together. Then you can dream of all the sunny lands to which those ships will go, the far away havens in which they will ride at anchor and all the strange people whom the sailors will see. Then there are melancholy dreams that must sometimes follow the ships sailing away, those ill-fated ships which sail away and never come back. Hemmed in by the low mountains of Northern Alabama, Lizzie Story missed the sight of the sea and the throng of visitors who came in the summer time to Watch Hill and stopped at the Larkin House, where she had at times worked with her mother, before she had graduated from the High School at Westerly, and come South to teach among her own people. But youth and hope were on her side, and she was in a section of country wonderfully new and beautiful to her. Her father and mother fled from Northern Alabama, where they were about to be sold apart in slavery times, and came to the far North, and finally found a country home at Watch Hill, Rhode Island. There they prospered and lived and died before Lizzie was twenty. But they had talked with her from her babyhood of the Sunny South, which they had left. They told her about the grand doings at Christmas times—how they all used to slip up to "De big house befo' day and ketch ole Mas' and ole Mis' Christmas gifs." Then there was a week off when the negroes had cabin dances, wore the cast-off finery of their masters and mistresses, and visited from plantation to plantation, just the same as other people of social natures. O! the glory of it all. How many times had Lizzie seen the reflection of it in her mother's face, when she related her story of the good old times and brought the warm, sunny South away up to Watch Hill, Rhode Island, where the winters are bleak and cold and the billows of the sea break on the cliffs at times with a fury terrible to behold. Then, too, there were visions of prodigality and magnificence, the glory of which Lizzie could not see as her mother did, who spoke volumes in that oft repeated sentence: "Whar I cum fum!" when she made comparisons between the scrimping and saving North and the open-handed and wasteful South. Somehow in that far away land of the Pilgrim fathers, those dusky parents from the land of the Cavaliers seemed to have forgotten all about the bitterness and hardship of slavery and had memory only for the glorious things of their former Southern home, to which after the war they were always going to return as soon as Lizzie got her education. But, alas! both of them in six months of each other, laid down and died before Lizzie got her diploma, but not before they had filled her heart with a love and a longing to go to her Southern home, which she had never seen except in dreams.

But at last, Lizzie Story came to the land of her fathers and brought with her all her New England training in thrift and her fortune of three thousand dollars, which her parents had left. With a part of this money she bought the old Huntley Place, near Greenbottom Inn. Lizzie Story had that turn of mind and energy that were bound to gather around her a goodly share of this world's goods. A little money, with foresight and energy, after the wrecks of the war, gave many a chance to get ahead in life, and Lizzie Story was among those who prospered at such times. She took an uncle and aunt to live with her. They had remained in the South till Abraham Lincoln's proclamation of freedom gave them their liberty. Lizzie Story, with her uncle and two hired men as work hands, successfully engaged in truck farming, while she herself taught the colored free school at Mercury. She was a born teacher and soon became a person of great note in that community. The poverty and the ignorance of the people appealed to her keen sympathies and she at once became a true missionary among them. She taught them much about housekeeping and a thousand little ways of living that the women had not had a chance to learn in slavery.

A few months after she began teaching, a woman who lived in a cabin near her died and left her boy alone in the world. His father was a Jew, and Bertie Stein, therefore, belonged to that large class of so-called negroes in the South, who belong wholly to no race. This boy had mixed Negro and Anglo-Saxon blood from his mulatto mother, and another blood that tells wherever it flows—that of Shem, from his father. He was one of Lizzie Story's pupils and near neighbor, and had interested her from the first by his winsome spirit. She took him home with her from his mother's grave, and they soon became great friends and companions, though there were six years difference between their birthdays. They were happy in their walks to and from school. Some mornings near Greenbottom Inn they met John Henry and Daphne McBride, whose story, as you know, I have already told you; but they did not meet often, for Lizzie and Bertie almost always passed the old Inn before John Henry and Daphne started to Buena Vista, where they attended the State Normal School, which at that time had not been transferred to old Greenbottom Inn, as it was destined to be a few years later. Bertie liked their morning walk to the school best, for as you went past the old Inn and wound around it to meet the sun on the old road, which goes on and on, nobody knows where, you had a more open stretch of country to see. The blue hills went up and down and lifted themselves away across the country until they reached the low mountains far away, that made a green wall all around the sky, and for Bertie there was always on those mountains in the morning sun, an enchantment, a wonderful glamour and play of illusions that made him happy with, perhaps, a vague longing and an indefinable wishing for something at the bottom of his heart and his happiness. When they reached the school, there were always groups of boys and girls at play on the grounds, but they always stopped their playing to run and say "Good morning. Miss Lizzie," for they loved her. They did not love Bertie Stein so well, for it was plain to them all that Miss Lizzie loved him the best of all her pupils, unless, perhaps, she loved little Harvey West as well, who came down from the mountain almost as wild and fierce as one of its catamounts, to all who crossed him, except Miss Lizzie, whom he loved dearly. Bertie was the head boy at school in everything, though he was not the oldest. He was Miss Lizzie's very little Squire of Knight Errantry, and the model of conduct for all the pupils. Sometimes the school discipline was hard to maintain, especially when the warm weather came on, one of those days came when seven devils seem to enter every boy's and girl's heart. But at such times Bertie was always to be counted on to help Miss Lizzie keep her patience and her temper, and therefore, her grip on the school. So the days, weeks and months passed by and then the time began to be numbered by years from the time of the first days when Lizzie Story and Bertie Stein began to pass by old Greenbottom Inn towards Mercury going to school. All the boys and girls who were classed with Bertie in time dropped out of school, while he kept on and in studies that were strangely out of proportion in the degree of advancement to the studies of the other pupils. Lizzie Story decided to send Bertie to college and she was fitting him herself. One September day after she had taught him six years, she sent him to Fisk University at Nashville, Tennessee. Her walks after that towards Mercury were lonely indeed, but one afternoon when she came from school, she found awaiting her a letter, which was the beginning of a correspondence that for four years was to be the chief pleasure of her life.

"Fisk University, Nashville, Tenn.,
Oct. 7, 18—

My Dear Miss Lizzie:—

You will pardon me, I trust, for waiting so long to write you again after the few lines sent upon my arrival in this City four weeks ago. I wanted to get settled in my school life before I wrote, so that I might be able to tell you all about myself and the school. I passed my examination for the Freshman Class. I got a condition in Greek, but I hope to get regular in my class before a great while. This place is very beautiful. Jubilee Hall is a fine building, and the great dining room in it, with its rows of Corinthian pillars and frescoed walls is a delightful place to come to when we are hungry. We have only a lunch at noon, and the dinner comes at half-past five. We are required to stay in our rooms and keep study hours from seven to nine at night and from nine to ten we are at liberty to visit or do what we wish until ten, when all lights must go out, and the students to bed. It is very jolly here and I like it. But let me tell you about Jubilee day, which we celebrated yesterday. It comes the 6th of October, and is kept in honor of the Jubilee Singers, who set out from the school on the 6th of October. We celebrated the day yesterday with a picnic at Clifton, a place two miles from here on a bluff by the Cumberland. It was a glorious day and almost too warm for the long walk. The Spence Cadets, the Student Military Company here, marched out and had a parade on the picnic grounds. The boys and girls had each other's company, that is those who wished to. We had a game of ball out there, but the ground was too rough for it. After the game we strolled about till dinner, at which time there was some speech making and the story of the singers was told. We had a delightful time, but we were all tired enough when we got home late in the afternoon. The boys say the next good thing to come is the Thanksgiving dinner and social that night. There are a great many students here from all parts of the country. I am very happy here but I get a little homesick at times and wish for you. The landscape scenery here is very beautiful, especially the valley that looks west from Jubilee Hall. But it is not so beautiful as it is around about old Greenbottom Inn. I shall be glad to hear from you soon.

As ever, yours,

Bertie Stein."

This letter was followed by others weekly, and Lizzie Story kept her hold on Bertie's life, all through his four years of college work. He grew into a beautiful young manhood, but always maintained much of that boyishness and simple trust that so characterized his relations to her from the first, and which made her at once his companion and absolute guide. In the spring of his senior year, Bertie's strength gave out and he suffered much from insomnia. One day early in May Miss Lizzie received a letter from him telling her that the doctor had advised him to come home and rest two weeks, but he said it was so near to commencement he would not come, but the second day after the receipt of that letter, Miss Lizzie was joyfully surprised by the arrival of Bertie himself. Two weeks that followed were blissful to her, all the more so, because it was a pleasure she had not expected. They were the last they were ever to have together with all the old ties unbroken, but Lizzie Story did not know that and the two weeks went by all too soon for her. On Thursday night before the day Bertie was to leave, he said at bed time,"Miss Lizzie,I want to see the sun rise over the hills and mountains once more towards Mercury, and I am going to climb the Northwest hill at daylight. Come with me, won't you?" "With pleasure, Bertie," she replied, and they both laid down to their sleep and the pleasant dreams that belong to young lives, where sorrow has not been. But sweet sleep and pleasant dreams come to an end in time. The night sped on and on and at last ushered in a new day, whose light brightened more and more upon Bertie and Lizzie as they climbed the hill northwest of the old Huntly farm in the early morning. The glory of May was everywhere. Already the hot weather had come, but at that early hour the air was blissfully cool,and every blade of grass and every leaf on bush and tree sparkled with the morning dew. In an adjoining pasture there was the tuneful jumble of the bell cow cropping the grass sweet and fine and all wet with dew, as she led the herd out for their long and blissful day in their pasture land. The sheep were moving off also in that formal procession which they always maintain and with a thousand tender bleats from the lambs and mothers. The crowing of the cocks and the songs of the birds came up the hillside sweet with all the joyous sounds of life. Lizzie and Bertie climbed slowly, speaking a word only now and then. It was life all too fresh and glorious

to be talked about, life only to be breathed
in with deep draughts and to be seen by
the eye as heavenly visions. Directly east
of the hill below in the valley old Greenbottom Inn nestled close to the earth in
the midst of its orchard full of the promise
of lucious fruit. The old slave road wound
its way by it towards the East as a yellow
thread, going on and on till it stopped by
the Atlantic Ocean, perhaps. On the top
of the hill at the brow of the woods, Lizzie
and Bertie sat down to rest and to look
backwards over the valley below them. Far
to the east the low mountains still made
for Bertie a green wall all round the sky
and in that glorious morning sunlight there
was still the play of illusions that belonged
to the happy mornings when he and Lizzie
went that way towards Mercury to school.
And all the valley south to the ''Three
Mountains'' and southeast to Monte Sano
was beautiful beyond words. Buena Vista,
peerless Buena Vista, with its fig trees, its
pomgranites, rich with promises of dapple
fruit, and its voluptuous roses blooming in
profusion, sat peacefully in the midst of
the valley like some great motherbird on
her summer nest. The sun came slanting
down the crest of Monte Sano, down the
cliffs of gray rocks covered with moss and

green ferns, creeping from the niches of the rocks. The Tennessee, with its yellow loop, went crawling into Northern Alabama, and then back into the State whose name it bears. Lizzie Story's heart was full to the brim of happiness. "O! it is so beautiful, almost like a beautiful dream," she said with suppressed emotions. "It is indeed," Bertie replied. "And yet, over beyond those green mountain walls there lies the world." "But why get over those green walls to find the world, Bertie? Why not find the world inside of this lovely valley?"

"It would be a world too small for me," he said with a low voice and a deep emotion new for him. He had not said truly what was in his heart. He had not said over those green walls love was drawing him with cords stronger than life. And she could not know it was so. She said no more, but dreamed on, and all her dreams were of Bertie Stein. He was the center of all the beauty, the glory and lovely life around her. And Bertie sat there dreaming also, but of another than Lizzie Story. He dreamed of one in the world beyond the green walls of the mountain, where the Cumberland winds around and washes with a horseshoe bend the Athens of the South. So love wrapped them both about in that sweet morning air, and for the hour at least created the world anew and made all things in it divine. And love is life, for on it the propagation of the race depends; still that same love is pain and is merciless. Nevertheless, one full, joyful day of it, perhaps, even one hour of it, such as Lizzie Story had on that hillside that early morning was worth a lifetime without it, worth all the sorrow that may have come afterwards because of that one hour of love unmodified in the momentary sweetness it gave to her existence.

Lizzie Story's life had been a simple one. She lived her first nineteen years of life in Rhode Island. It was what every negro girl's life is in that land. She mixed freely in church and school with the white boys and girls. There was never an act of unkindness in all her life from them to her on account of race distinction. They were friendly and kind and every right was granted to her, but for all that she grew up among them an alien. The things of life touched her only on the outside. She was the only negro in the high school the four years she was there. She attended the class ball at the time of her graduation, and the boys of the class danced with her, just as they did with the other girls of the class, but that was essentially all the social life Lizzie Story ever knew. She came to Northern Alabama soon after her graduation from the High School at Westerly, Rhode Island. She taught the district school at Mercury, and that with the truck farming, which she most successfully carried on at the same time, consumed all her time and energy. Bertie Stein came to her when he was eleven years old, and had filled all her life and soul. She loved him and lived for him. At first she loved him because he was a winning and loving little boy in her school. Then she loved him more because she adopted him into her home, sympathized with him and became a part of all that made up his life with its abundant promise. She had never stopped to analyze her love for him to see what kind it was. Indeed, there was no necessity for that. Her's was that good love, which has no cause for concealment or shame. It was the love she would have given the man she married, the child she might have borne, and the love she gave to Christ, her Lord and Redeemer. And if there is any one shocked at such a moralization, let him tell to the world of a good love for a human being, in which any one of the three I mention may be left out, or put his hand on the exact spot where these three unite and make separate and distinct links. All good loves of the human heart lie inside of these three, which are a trinity. It was only in September, during those blissful and last days of vacation, before he returned to college for his senior year, that Lizzie Story ever began to think of Bertie Stein in a new sense. He was so manly then, so gallant and lover-like in all their walks and life together. He was then so much taller than she was. The six years' difference in their birthdays did not seem so great as formerly.

On the morning he started for college. She said: "You must leave off calling me Miss Lizzie, Bertie. The old Mercury district school days are over long ago."

"Are they?" he said laughingly. Then he put his arms around her and kissed her, saying, "You will be my Alabama, my inspiration of life and my Miss Lizzie for ever and ever."

It was done and said with all the old boyish playfulness, yet with such a fervor and decision that Lizzie Story's heart beat with emotions that had never stirred there before. Bertie felt and meant all he said, but it was truer then unmodified than it

ever was afterwards. That very next week
in the rush of the new school year, when
the old and the new students were coming
in, the whole current of life was to change
for Bertie Stein, the joint son of Abraham
and some heathen negro in Africa. What
a marvelous thing is life and the influence
of many centuries that center in and direct
one man's life and give it its affinities for
another life. From the neighborhood of
the Arabian Gulf over the plains of Meso-
potamia, from Egypt by the way of Mt.
Sinai and Palestine, a current of life, together with another from the jungles of
Africa, from Fetich dances and idol wor-
ship had been creeping on for four thousand years gathering up those influences
and affinities that were destined to be united in Bertie Stein, the Negro-Jew, and
consume his life in the fervid intensity of
love for another life, which his had been
travelling to meet all those thousand years.
Great God! and for what purpose? To
give the world one more riddle?

Fisk University is a co-education college. In the beautifully frescoed dining-
room of Jubilee Hall, Bertie Stein was seat-
ed at a table where there was an exceedingly attractive new student. She was from
Louisiana, having studied in the schools

at New Orleans, and had come to Fisk University mainly for its excellent musical advantages. She was a Creole, she said. Most all the mulattoes, so they say, are Creoles, who come from Louisiana. To Bertie Stein, Stella Jerome was a divinity from the first hour he saw her. He had gone with a different college girl each year— the second year with two different ones, and got through all the school-boy love episodes with both before the commencement of that year. Nobody thought his fervor about Stella was serious. It was plain that she was not much in love with him, but this time in Bertie's case the real passion had come to his soul. The school year sped on towards its close and Bertie was still persistent in his love suit. He had asked Stella to marry him a dozen times or more, and she had said no as many times, but Bertie had no intention of giving the matter up. She had strange moods at times, and was evidently morbid over some matter. She clung to Bertie all through the year for two reasons. It is most convenient and the fashion for each girl who can to have some young man to depend on for a regular escort and to pay those little attentions at all times so gratifying to the female heart. Then, more than that, Stella found Bertie's love something to cling to at times when she was in low spirits and in moments of secret desperation. She told him the story of her life once, making allusions which he did not understand, but which might have been plainer to him if he had been less pure at heart. She saw his innocence and regretted her confidence. When he questioned her for the meaning of some things she said, she turned the matter off and told him more of the stepmother, who, she said, had cruelly wronged her when she was very young. Bertie fancied the beatings and desolate childhood that had been hers. He was all the more tender to her and was eloquent with his plea to be allowed to make the rest of her life easy. Stella smiled through tears at his enthusiasm, and in her secret soul she would at that moment at least have given a world to be able to love him and to be worthy of his love. One day soon afterwards she stood at the table tearing a letter to bits and dropping them in her apron pocket as the students were coming in to dinner. When Bertie came in she whispered to him as he sat down beside her: "I will say yes if you will marry me commencement day and take me to Germany to study music for a year."

"Don't joke about that," he said.

"I am not joking," she replied.

Bertie was glorified. It was just four weeks to commencement, but the doctor had told him the day before that he must go away and be quiet for two weeks or he would come down with a fever before the four weeks were out. He had been thinking all the morning of going home for the two weeks if he had to go anywhere. Stella's whispered message had decided him at once. It was necessary to see Lizzie Story without delay. But the next day when he went to make his good-bye call on Stella he found her in a most unaccountable mood. She took back her engagement the very first thing, and pretended that she was joking. When Bertie said with such a tone of reproach, "What have I done that has made me deserve such joking as this?" she burst into a violent fit of weeping. But she suddenly ceased and said defiantly, "No, I was not joking; I meant every word I said, but I tell you, Bertie Stein, if I keep my engagement and marry you it will not be six months till you will wish you had not married me. I am telling you what I know will be true, and now if you wish me to marry you, I will do it, but don't forget that I wanted to back out of the bargain.''

''I wish you to marry me,'' said Bertie doggedly, and ''I would wish it if I knew it was to be only for one day, so great is my love for you.''

Stella was moved to tenderness by his passionate speech, but she at once covered her feelings by assumed gaiety. The hour allotted them to visit according to the school regulations came to its close and her nervousness and anxiety returned.

''Do you really wish me to keep this foolish engagement?'' she said.

He was half vexed and replied, ''Yes, I do. Why did you make it if you did not want to keep it, especially when you knew it is what I desired more than anything else in the world?''

''Why did I make it? Let me tell you with the piano.''

She sat down and played to him with precision and great feeling, but she was not an artist and could not convey much of a message through a piano, perhaps. But Bertie was still less an artist than she, and he would not have understood her through music, even if she had been able to express herself that way.

"What did that music tell you?" she said.

"Nothing," he replied. "It was very sweet and sad. What is the name of the piece?"

"Gottschalk's Last Hope," she said.

"O! I see; I was your last hope, your last chance," he said laughingly.

The bell rang for supper and they went into the dining-room together along with that gay and happy throng of young life, whose feet never grow weary of coming and whose hunger is never satisfied, though the years pass on and on.

The next day Bertie Stein went to Northern Alabama to see Miss Lizzie and to rest. The two weeks went by pleasantly, but Bertie was not free from his restlessness anl sleepless nights that had so told on his strength during the past month. He had not been able to say to Lizzie Story the thing that had been uppermost in his heart all the two weeks and which had brought him home to say, much more than the matter of rest. So at that early hour before the heat came on, when they sat at the top of the hill dreaming and talking as of old, after a long silence he broke into their dreaming by saying, "Miss Lizzie, I have something to say to you, which I have been trying to say every day these two weeks, but it is so different from anything we ever talked about before I could not do it.''

Lizzie Story's heart was tumultuous, just as many a woman's heart has been before when she heard such a prelude.

"You told me when I left for school last fall that you were going to give me the day I graduated four hundred dollars for every year we spent together on this farm. I want to marry that very day and go to Europe for a year. I was only engaged two days before I came here, and you must not blame me for not writing about it to you. I love Stella better than I do my own life and soul, and do not believe I could live without her. She has promised to marry me if I would do it commencement day and take her to Europe for a year. May I do it, Miss Lizzie?''

He had his eyes turned down the valley and he did not see Lizzie Story stagger as if from a blow, nor how she held on to the tree against which she leaned, that she might not faint.

"Tell me all about Stella, Bertie," she said hysterically. He was so absorbed he did not notice her emotion. He began to tell her of Stella, his star of the first magnitude. For half an hour he talked on, tell-

ing her story as she had told it to him,
adding all the halo and superior virtues
which love ever adds to such real facts as
there are. Lizzie Story was not convinced
of the superiority of Stella Jerome as Bertie imagined, nor of the wisdom of a marriage made upon such conditions, but in
this gain of time, when she did not need to
talk, she fought her battle of life and
saved her soul in its death agony from
Bertie's sight.

"Yes, Bertie, I will give you the money
commencement day, as I said I would,"
she replied, when he ceased his talking of
Stella. There was something in her voice
that Bertie had never heard before. He
looked up at her wonderingly and instinctively felt that he had wounded her. She
smiled and said in answer to his look,
"You see, Bertie, you have so surprised
me and you have been all mine so long, I
do not know how to give you up all at
once."

A great lump came in his throat. "O!
Miss Lizzie," he replied, embracing her
with all of his old boyish fondness, "you
do not have to give me up, I am sure you
will love Stella. Then you will have two
of us instead of one. We will just be your
Stella and your Bertie forever."

"Yes," she said, "you will be mine forever and forever."

He did not notice that Stella was left out of the everlasting compact, nor did he know that he had wounded a heart nigh unto death. They lingered on the hill top a while longer, talking about the future, but somehow both felt that a gulf had suddenly slipped in between them. Lizzie Story readily assented to all arrangements Bertie suggested about the coming year, but he was disappointed because she did not question him more about Stella. They soon felt it was time to go home. The sun was high in the heavens now and the heat of the day was on. They talked about the most commonplace things as they went down the hillside. Much of the glamor was gone from the valley and in the glare of the sun the enchantment so apparent in the distance from the hill top in the early morning was gone. Near the noon hour Lizzie Story stood on the rude platform facing the little shed called the depot near old Greenbottom Inn and gave Bertie Stein an affectionate good-bye. He was in high spirits. When the sun went down he knew he would be in sight of the city where his love was. He was too happy and too self-centered in that hour to think that there

might be a heart in the world with sorrow
in it, and Lizzie Story was kind to the last.
She watched the train out of sight and returned Bertie's last wave of the handker-
chief. He did not know the sadness of farewell. His face was towards the North and
love was the magnetic needle that drew
him on. He reached Nashville and the University grounds just as the sun set. The
college campus is delightful at that hour
in the warm spring weather. The evening
meal was over and the prayers were said.
Away to the west there was a violet mist
on the hills behind which the sun was setting. In Jubilee Square the girls were
promenading on the walk-ways or sitting
in groups on the grassy lawn. Some of the
boys were playing ball in Victoria Square,
while others about Livingstone Hall were
in groups delighting themselves in banters,
guys and light talk, as only school boys can
do. The air everywhere was sweet with
the perfume of flowers and all the gay
young life of the school was out in the
campus taking in the sweet breath of life
before the study bell called them in for the
night. There was only a few more evening
hours of this kind after Bertie's return and
then commencement day came and scattered the students far and wide.

Three days after commencement, just at dark, a strange white man, who had been hanging about Jubilee Square all the afternoon, as if watching for some one, drew near Jubilee Hall. Nearly all the students were gone and all over the college campus there was a strange quietness, where but a few days before there was a busy stir of life. There were signs of disorder, scattered rubbish, withered evergreens and flowers—pitiful signs of wasted life, that are ever apparent after the festival is over. Old Martin was sweeping the halls and carrying out all sorts of trash to be carted away when a stranger came up and asked him to tell Stella Jerome that he wanted to speak to her.

"Why, boss! she's done married and gone to Europe three days ago."

"What!" exclaimed the stranger excitedly.

"Why, yas; it wuz a big surprise to all de folks might near. A few knowed it befo dey cumed out to git married on de flatform arter de speaking wuz over. Dey's gone to Europe to travel and study a year, and den Bertie Stein, dat's Mis' Stella's husband, is cumin' back here and gwine into a sto' to do business. Mis' Stella got a mighty nice young man, Boss."

137

"A nice young man to hell," said the stranger, who turned away and left old Martin looking amazed. At that very hour the two young people missing from Jubilee Hall were out on the deck of a great ocean steamer, watching a full moon come up over the broad expanse of the sea. Stella had been down to the Gulf from New Orleans and knew what the ocean was like, but Bertie had only seen the mountains and valleys of Northern Alabama and Tennessee. The wonderful mystery of the sea and the moonlight on the surging waters gave him feelings that he had never felt before. There was in his heart, perhaps, a sense of awe and vagueness of longing that he used to feel when he saw the play of illusions on the mountains in the morning sunlight when he went towards Mercury in North Alabama to school with Miss Lizzie. His thoughts went backward to her with loyal tenderness, and he wondered if she was thinking of him. All at once he began to wonder why she did not come to see him graduate and married. She sent the check instead of bringing it the day before commencement, as he had expected. She wrote that she was not able to get off from home. Bertie was much disappointed, but he was in such a whirl of events he could not stop to think of the matter. But out on the ocean in the moonlight he talked the matter with Stella and wondered what could have hindered her coming. But Stella was wiser in matters of the heart than Bertie, and told him that his Miss Lizzie did not come, perhaps, because she did not want to see another woman marry a man she wanted to marry herself. Bertie laughed and told her that her guess for the ridiculous would pass all others. But his trip across the ocean would not have been so happy if he had seen Lizzie Story when she turned her back on the depot after his train passed from sight, when he bade her good-bye. But he could not know. She smiled then, was her old happy self to his eyes and wished him happiness. It was when he was gone that she turned a sorrowful face towards home, and with lagging steps that were new to her. She went out of her way homeward that day slowly taking the path further up the hill and passed close by the colored State Normal and Industrial School, which had the year before been moved up from Buena Vista, when old Greenbottom Inn was purchased for a teachers' home and a number of new buildings were erected for the students. As she passed Palmer Hall she saw some of the students looking longingly out of the windows into the sunshine. Farther along the hillside eastwards, the work-shops were in full swing of activity, and there was heard the dull thumping of machinery under the great civilizing force of steam. Skilled negro labor on that hillside with hope and youth all before it was being prepared for the advancement of the world, infinitely more than the world had any idea of. And even more significant, in Palmer Hall, from which place came longing looks through the windows for the freedom of the sunshine and the shade of the campus, there were forces at work more silently than those of the bustling and whirring workshops, but infinitely more wide-reaching in effect. It was all a promise and a prophecy of the negro's freedom and redemption. Lizzie Story gave a sigh of gladness for it all, out of her sad heart, as she passed by the school. Along the path where she walked the cactus grew by the thousands among the rocks. They were in bloom with their yellow corrollas fringed by a thousand hair-like needles. The gray lizards full of happy and lazy life basked in the sun and ran in and out among the cactus. Lizzie Story stopped to look at these little creatures so low in the scale of life, and without sorrow. She felt glad for the fortune of gay life allotted to them. Somehow the sense of compassion was deep in her at that moment. Perhaps it was because she was so sorry for herself. When she reached home she looked into a mirror and ran from the face she saw—a face from which the first bloom of youth had gone out. Into her heart there rushed a sudden sense of shame and guilt. "You old woman, to want that boy's heart and love," that face from the mirror had said. All night long a second Miss Lizzie accused and shamed her. Even in the darkness she would hide her face under the sheet, when the unrelenting accuser mocked her and reminded her that the boy had loved her from child to manhood in the sweetest innocence, but in all his life he had never thought of her except as Miss Lizzie, his best friend, his teacher, his sister and his mother, all in one. But love is a creature, who has no age and no possible consideration for incongruities, whatever may be the strictures of the one who entertains him.

So it came about while Bertie Stein that evening laid down to sweet fancies of love and happiness, Lizzie Story tossed all night long on her bed, with a breast that could not stop its aching and with a heart that could not cease from bleeding and yet could not die.

CHAPTER II.

Far in the afternoon of a warm day early in July, two travelers from a distant land were drawing near the "Eternal City."

Bertie Stein and his bride were crossing the Campagna, the wide plain of the Tiber and of the most varied and thrilling history of all past civilization.

There had been a passing thunderstorm in the morning, leaving behind it pure air and a tender light over all the landscape. The blue haze on the mountains, under bluer skies, the soft sunshine, the green fields, the loaded vineyards and the wide-spreading chestnut trees, were all faithful to the fair fame of Italy.

Here and there they saw sculptured and broken columns of marble, which spoke of Rome in all her past glory, when her empire stretched from England to India. They passed by the old Claudian aqueduct which brought water from the Albian Hills to the city of Romulus and Remus, and soon the spires of the city itself began to gleam in the distance.

The next few days in Rome were days never to be forgotten by Bertie. He stood in the old Forum, where Cicero gave utterance to some of his immortal orations a hundred years before Christ was born. In imagination Bertie saw the Roman audiences, under the spell of their immortal orator. Julius Caesar, who had led the armies of Rome in triumph through Gaul and across the sea to the land of the Druids, and Pompey, who had carried the Roman eagles in all the East, were there, subject to the power of Cicero. Mark Antony, the debauchee, destined to perish with Cleopatra, for the moment forgot all thought of riot and disorder listening to the man who was swelling with vain glory in his conscious power over the audience before him. Virgil, Horace, Sallust and Seneca forgot their boyish pranks, and listened spellbound to the man who was touching the power of genius lying hidden in those four boys—poetical romance and song in two, the genius of history and philosophy in the others.

Leaving the Forum, he went along the street, past the temple of Jupiter and came to the mighty arches of the Temple of Peace, reared by Vespasian to commemorate his victory over the Jews, those

brought captives to Rome, having worked
in the claypits making the bricks to build
the walls, which were to hand down
through all time their own humiliation.

And near this were the time-worn stones
of the arch of Titus, telling the history of
the destroyed nation of those same people
over whom Vespasian triumphed, and yet
a people whom neither he nor Titus could
utterly break nor destroy from the earth.

Then, exalted on a hill, above all other
sights, stood the Capitol, once the most
significant of all marble piles, and from
which went out that famous decree that
all the world should be taxed.

The Coliseum, and other sights of renown, were all seen in turn. The Rome
of the college imagination was banished;
but the real Rome of the Caesars and St.
Paul was traversed through and through.

Later other famous Italian cities were
visited, and every day was filled with the
keenest interest and happiness for Bertie
Stein. Stella enjoyed the travel and scenes
of interest also; and, in the excitement and
novelty of foreign life, she did not fall into
her moody spells so often. She was gracious to Bertie, and strove to be affectionate to him, so that he did not see that she
wearied of his devotions at times.

Early in the fall they went to Germany and settled in Berlin for the winter. Stella began her study of music at once, and for six months worked hard. She was an advanced piano player, and had a certain brilliancy that attracted some attention among the students with whom she came in contact. She enjoyed the life and her surroundings.

Bertie traveled from place to place much of the time, coming back to Stella after a brief absence full of enthusiasm and full of generous love for her.

When they had been married eleven months a baby boy came to them and Bertie was glorified. As soon as the mother became strong they turned their steps homeward and finally got back to Nashville after an absence of sixteen months. Burton Story Stein was five months old.

They rented and furnished a small house and began housekeeping with high hopes for the future, and for one month not a cloud crossed their happy sky.

One day in November Stella was walking eastward along Church street, and just beyond the Nicholson House she looked up the short avenue that leads up to ex-President James K. Polk's old mansion. There was a fakir there selling patent medicines and haranguing the crowd about him with tales of the wonderful cures of his medicines.

In the crowd she thought she caught the glimpse of a face looking straight at her that sent a thrill of terror through her heart; but in the shift and surging of the crowd the face was lost and she passed on, thinking the glimpse had only given her a resemblance of one she knew. She went onward through the throngs of the street and finally into the great store of Lubecks on Market Square. When she had made her purchases and passed out she did not notice a man who stood at the doorway waiting for her until she heard the low greeting, "Howdy, Stella," in a voice well known to her. She was almost paralyzed with sickening fear and dread.

"For God's sake, leave me, Harrison Jerome," she gasped, in a low and agonized voice.

"Not much I wont," he replied. "Come on, I am going home with you. It's no use, Stella, I have come after you. That slip you gave me is no go."

"Come on and let me talk to you," she said, and led him to the great suspension bridge which spans the Cumberland to East Nashville. She knew that they would attract the least attention standing on the bridge where people often stop to look about them.

"Harrison," she said, turning a face to him full of pain, full of a plea for pity and mercy, "I am married to a nice man and have a child," and the wretched woman pleaded her case, going over all the circumstances from her childhood unto that hour. When she spoke of the stepmother and the bargain made for money that bound her to him when she was too young to know that the thing which seemed an advancement of her situation at the time was only a degradation and wicked sale, that he should not press to her ruin, when she was struggling for the better life, he was angered by the allusion and sneeringly said, "Your year in Fisk University, indeed, I see has greatly advanced your ethics. You seemed pretty well satisfied with the sale for five years."

"Yes, I was; I loved you," she said meekly. "I did not take the steps I did for the lack of love for you then nor now, but for God's sake, Harrison, go away and leave me."

The man before her was not without some kindness of heart, but he was long callous in sin, and he did not draw nice

147

dictinctions in certain matters. There is a certain kind of marriage custom in the South of long standing by which a white man does not lose caste and the octoroon women generally chosen are by many of the ignorant negroes thought to be advanced. No license of law or the sanction of priests make these unions, but they are common. Harrison Jerome did not feel that he was urging an unjust claim, and the fact that love was still alive was sufficient with him. The girl's new notions would soon give way, he thought. Stella had been concerning herself with questions of life that had never entered his soul. He did not know the straits of the woman pleading with him, and he would not yield. He gave her choice of meeting him at the depot at eight that night, to leave for Louisiana, or his giving Bertie Stein the whole story with a bullet for interest if he interfered. Stella knew Harrison Jerome too well to refuse, and she gave him her word to obey.

She left him on the bridge and went home. It was a miserable day for her. Bertie came to supper as usual, and when he started back for the night hours, he kept open, kissed Stella and Story as usual. Suddenly she resolved to tell him the whole

story and beg him for mercy. She showed
by her manner that she had something on
her mind that troubled her, and he said
with all the lavishness of his heart, "What
is it, Stella, mine?"

The confession was a terrible one to
make, and she could not bring herself to do
it. "Are you in a hurry?" she said falter-
ingly.

"Yes, but I can stop if you wish me."

"Well—no, I will wait till you come
back."

Bertie Stein had a kind heart, one that
would have been sore unto death had she
told him all, but his love for her was very
great. He would not have forsaken her,
and through him she might have been
saved. But the one chance to tell him
passed forever. She was a proud woman
and had had too much of his great love and
admiration to live with him with anything
less. When he was gone she sank down in
misery and despair. "I am lost," she said.
"I might as well go first as last. I was a
fool to have ever thought I could escape."
She knew Harrison would be in that house
before Bertie returned if she was not at the
depot by eight o'clock, and the scandal
given to the city. She cradled Story to his
rest for the night, and at seven she was

ready to leave the house. She wrote Bertie a letter and told him the whole story and begged him to forgive her, and then she stood a long time by Story's crib, sinking to her knees at last with a piteous moan and laid her face against his.

"Oh! God, I cannot help it all now. I am not to blame," she moaned into the ear of the sleeping child. The clock struck the half past hour of warning and she arose from her knees and went out into the dark.

Away across the city to the northwest on Fort Gillum, Jubilee Hall was flaring with a hundred blinking lights from the rooms of the students. An indescribable pang of pity for herself went through Stella's heart. She could not help feeling that she was in a tangle of sin and shame that was not much of her making, and the memory of all her struggles for the higher ideals of life rushed anew upon her when she looker over to those lights of Jubilee Hall where she had started upon the new path of life with earnest resolves, though the manner of her starting was a great blunder.

All at once there came to her mind a terrible temptation. She was young, and all the splendid instincts of animal life made her shudder at the thought of death, but her desperation was so great that a sudden madness caused her to rush once more with a half resolve towards the suspension bridge over the Cumberland.

When she reached Market Square she stopped and drew from her pocket an old letter, which she had and tore a blank slip from the envelope and wrote on it, "Dear Bertie, I have decided to go a different road, Stella Stein," and pinned the note to her bosom. She reached the bridge and walked out upon it to the place where she had stood with Harrison Jerome in the morning sunlight. The night was now closed down upon the muddy river, and the darkness brooding over its waters was only relieved by the flickering gas lamps, that vistaed the streets along the river's banks.

The stately flow of the Cumberland along the bed where it had moved for more than a thousand years, perhaps, in its change-lessness seemed a mockery to the petty events and wild passions of the millions of men who had lived by its banks. Above it on the bridge Stella Jerome, the creole from Louisiana, stood at the climax of her life, and almost at the end of its struggles. All of the events that led her up to that hour and place were too common, and in some instances too much to be condemned to allow her the color of romance. Moreover, a judgment already passed on the whole class from which she came is such that would not allow the possibility of the many exceptions of an original high nature of which she was one, so that the wretched woman on the bridge struggling with the fear of death and the shame of life, was robbed of all that is heroic and epic in her final wrestle with fate. For a long time she walked slowly to and fro on the bridge irresolute in her purpose, but feeling certain that she would at last do what she came to do. Again and again she stopped and looked down into the dark waters in which so many wild and stormy hearts after one last calculation, one last resolve, one last thought and one last shiver of dread, had stilled their beatings forever and forever. But when the fascination grew to be almost irresistible, Stella would draw away and put off the last act just a little longer. In her fever of half delirium at one moment she carried Story in her arms, then she walked with Bertie, and Harrison Jerome's face was close to hers and she knew she loved that face, and finally under the impulse to get away from that love she stopped short with a move-

ment so apparent in its purpose a policeman who had been watching her shouted
out sternly, "What are you about there?"
Whether from fright the balance was lost
or a last resolve was reached will never be
determined. Certainly it was not like a de-
liberate and fearless plunge. There was
one wild cry and a splash. In the stillness
of the night the river was heard moving
on with lapping on the banks as if only a
pebble had dropped from the bridge on its
bosom. An hour afterwards the form of
a beautiful woman with her wet clothes
clinging closely to her lay on the table of
the morgue at the police station. The long
hair was disheveled and dripping. Her
fair face, dress and name kept back any
suspicion that she belonged to the negro
race. The matron of the police station dis-
covered the note pinned to the bosom, and
handed it to a reporter of "The American," who was rapidly getting his story
from the policeman who saw the last act.
The matron folded the hands of the dead
woman across her breast, whose storm was
over. On the face there was no trace of
sorrow or sin or fear. It was all peace,
meekness and innocence.

While the police matron was doing the
last little acts of kindness for Stella Stein,

Bertie was within a few steps of their home. The house was as still as death, except for the soft breathing in Story's crib, and the moment he came in a sudden sense of fear that something was wrong rushed over him. He saw Stella's letter addressed to him and with trembling hands tore it open and read it. Bertie Stein's heart died within him when he read that last message from Stella. He was too stunned to think, and he sat down by the fire that burned lower and lower, flickered and went out, where the embers still glowed awhile and then turned to gray ashes. The dark hour before day came, and then the gray dawn with its chill, came creeping on from the East and into the room where Bertie sat and kept watch over his dead heart. By and by steps were heard on the porch, and there came to the stunned watcher within a quick sensation of life—life stifled with a great sense of expectation. He thought it might be Stella coming back. It was the milkman leaving his daily supply at the door. The rapid steps of some early passenger echoed along the pavement and died away in the distance. The gray dawn crept stealthily away to the West and the sun came up over East Nashville and the great white Capitol, Tennessee's pride and glory.

The murmur of life, which began with the tread of many feet, the rumble of carts over the stony streets in the early dawn, increased, till the thunder of steam cars, the shout of the newsboy and the cry of the hucksters became a mighty roar of life in all the city. Story slept on until late in the morning. He roused at last and made that usual demand for his breakfast that a youngster five months old will make when his breakfast is not forthcoming as he thinks it should. Bertie cautiously opened the door wide enough to put out his hand and draw in the milk bottle left by the milkman. He filled Story's bottle and gave it to him, and that youngster let it be known that he had the whole of the satisfaction of life by a vigored smacking and sucking of his bottle. Bertie's senses became more acute and his mind clearer by action in attending to Story's wants. He drew the window blinds further down lest some one might see in the house—might see the blight which had come into it. O! the shame of it all! He sat down once more in silence. Once he thought he heard a newsboy in the distance cry, "Paper—all about Stella Stein's suicide." He leaped from his seat with his ears strained and a tight sensation about the heart, that made it feel as if it would burst. Once more, came the cry further away, "Paper! all about the suicide—paper!" Then his eyes fell on the letter of last night and he sat down once more in a stupor. About eight in the morning there came the tramping of many feet upon the porch at Bertie Stein's door. His partner in business was early at the morgue, and when Bertie Stein did not come he guessed the truth—that he had not seen the morning papers. Bertie opened the door, and when he saw the black ambulance at the gate he remembered the newsboy's cry and knew that Stella was come back. Then there came a darkness and a blank. The shadows of the afternoon were on when he awoke from the blank of the morning and the house was full of friends and tender hearts.

The next night at the Chattanooga depot Bertie passed through the crowd of hack and expressmen, who were vociferously shouting their offers of service and then by the gatekeeper to the train, whose engine was already belching forth steam and impatience to the passengers, who were hurrying in. The conductor gave his final signal to the engineer, the shout "All aboard," to the passengers and they were off to the South. On and on the great iron steed sped through the night, making impatient stops here and there for passengers to get off and on. For some of those getting off there were glad cries of welcome, and the lights of home shining in the distance, where there were warmth and good cheer within. But those taking the train had their backs on the home lights, and there were tearful good-byes that followed the train out of the station on its mad race. In the middle of the smoking car there was a small partition on which were posted, "This compartment for colored passengers." In this retreat Bertie Stein sat throughout the night, holding in his arms a little fluffy bundle of sleeping life. When at last the train reached the station at Greenbottom Inn it was not far from day, but the darkness still hung thick on the mountains. Bertie made his way to his old home and Miss Lizzie. When he knocked old Aunt Joicy said, "Who is dat?" with a voice that plainly showed she was in no sense pleased with a caller at that untimely hour. Bertie answered by giving the old signal of a double knock that belonged to bygone days, when he was out. "Lawd bless my soul, if 'tain't Bertie," exclaimed Aunt Joicy, as she hobbled out of bed. In the next room there was also a low cry akin to gladness and pain. After a moment of hastily dressing, Miss Lizzie opened the door and the light shone fully into Bertie's face. It was the first time she had seen it since that day two years before when they parted at the train. "O! Bertie! Bertie! what is the matter and what is this?" she cried.

"It's just Story and I come to you, Miss Lizzie." She saw his broken heart in his face, and heard it in the moan of his voice. She gathered him and the sleeping child in her arms and wept over them. He wept also. They were the first tears he had shed. He gave Miss Lizzie Stella's letter and a crumpled newspaper account, which told her the whole story—all of the story which he himself knew.

Sorrow of any kind rarely kills anybody, and for young people time is a great healer. Bertie took up life once more at old Greenbottom Inn. Miss Lizzie could not suppress the joy she felt in getting him back again, and to stay, as he told her from the first. She thought after the first few days that his sorrow was not very deep. Not a word of complaint or a moan of the heart ever escaped him, but as the time went by, Lizzie Story saw that she was mistaken— that the Bertie of the old days had not come back, nor would ever come. He was now a man with a sorrow which would color his life to the grave. He entered into the farm life with interest, but there was a passiveness and almost indifference apparent in his inner spirit which troubled Miss Lizzie, and she put forth every effort to arouse him to new motives in life. In years he was yet scarcely a man. He was sensible of her effort for him and responded in some measure, but she had to learn that the bond for a deep sympathy between them must have a new basis. He was no more the boy, Bertie Stein. Story was one common bond between them, and drew them close to each other. A chance lecture heard upon the environment and some peculiar circumstances of the negro boys and girls of the South that grew out of the institution of slavery now passed away, interested Bertie in sociological questions and finally led him into some attempts and organizations to better the condition of the boys and girls of Buena Vista. Lizzie Story entered into all his efforts with zeal and money, partly because she was interested, but more because they actively took Bertie away from himself, and in time they were as united and as dependent upon each as in the old Mercury school days. When he had been home nearly three years, after a conversation one day touching upon several phases of the philosophy of life, he suddenly asked Miss Lizzie why she had never married, and if she had never loved any one. She was so surprised she did not answer at first, but evasion on any subject was not the rule with them. Finally she said, "Yes, I loved one man more than my life. I did not marry him because he loved some one else and married her." She went out of the room at once and left Bertie astounded. He could not think at first whom she could ever have so loved. At once Stella's remark on the steamer that first night out from New York came back to him, and then he remembered all the incidents of that early morning on the hill, when he told of his great love for Stella, and then the whole truth flashed upon him and shocked him at first. That was in October, and as the months went by the thought that she loved him in that way became more and more pleasant to him. He became almost a changed man towards her, and the change at first was so reserved, Lizzie Story's heart ached and she shed bitter tears in secret because of her folly in letting him suspect the truth, as she now knew he did. That winter was a mild one, and in February the peach trees were in bloom and the ground was yellow everywhere with dandelions. There came a sunny day towards the last of the month when the thermometer was almost up to summer heat. The farmers were plowing and all the advanced movements of spring were everywhere apparent. But Miss Lizzie on that day was unusually low-spirited and cross. There were many lambs that season, and on the night before the dogs which had been making great havoc among the farmers' sheep, broke in Lizzie Story's fold on the Northwest hill pasture and killed many lambs and old sheep. She had been out all morning on the hillside looking after her sheep, and her vexation was complete when she came home near noon to see a fine young cherry tree hacked all around by the ever-energetic young Story, and her feelings were not molified by this scene, turning out to be another episode of George Washington and the hatchet. Indeed, the ever-resourceful youngster showed not only by the very features of his face, but by his most persistent version of the cause of the ruined cherry tree that his lineage went far beyond that of the Father of our country, indeed, all the way back

to Annanias himself, for although seen in
the very act of "chopping wood," he de-
clared that he did not cut the cherry tree,
but when pushed to the last extreme he
admitted that his "naughty hatchet" cut
it. Bertie was very tender to Miss Lizzie
all that afternoon, and almost insensibly
made her forget all the worries of the day.
When night came, he went to bed early,
so that he might get up after a few hours'
sleep and go to the hillside to watch there
for the return of the dogs. They would not
make their raid before midnight. When
he got ready to go, Miss Lizzy was dressed
and ready to go with him. He advised her
not to go out, but secretly he was very glad
to have her company. It would be lonely
out there on that hill in the dark, and there
was another reason why her company was
desirable. It was a warm spring night, but
they were both well wrapped up and both
had a gun. It was a beautiful star-light
night. They took their position not far
from the sheep and waited in silence for
the coming of the enemy. They did not
talk much, but they both felt that they
were very near each other. It was the heart
speaking to the heart. Their faces were
turned eastward, where there was a dark
wall all around the sky. The night was

very clear, and the twinkling of the myriad host of stars was like the throbbing of the mighty heart of the universe. The North star shone with a pale tinge of red, while the Great Bear, flaming with light, swung outwardly from it a little to the east. Capella was like yellow gold, and Aldebaran was fiery red. Sirius, the brightest star in all the heavens, flashed with a whiteness and a steely glitter like some mammoth diamond. A little to the right of glittering Sirius the whole constellation of mighty Orion, the hunter, split in two by the equinoctial line, hung wedge-shaped in the fathomless universe, and farther than the eye could reach the milky way stretched out.

In the stillness of the night and the fanciful sense of the glide of the stars above, they almost felt the roll of the world eastward. Slowly up over the dark wall around the sky the moon crept in her last quarter, now too decrepit with age to light up the mountains for Bertie Stein, and put upon them that play of illusions which had been there for him in his happy boyhood days. It was only a melancholy light, which it shed from a life that was almost spent. Neither Bertie nor Miss Lizzie spoke, as they sat there and looked upon it all. They were too near the great heart of the Eternal One for much speech at that hour. Bertie's hand had found its way into Miss Lizzie's, and they both sat there on the hillside dreaming once more, but this time of each other.

"Miss Lizzie," Bertie said at last, "it was on this hillside that I told you my first love story, and I now wish you to hear my second." Then Bertie told Lizzie Story the oldest story in the world, but to her the newest and sweetest she ever heard. It did not have in it the fiery breath that breathed through his love when he told her about Stella Jerome. It could not have that, but it had enough in it to satisfy the heart of Lizzie Story. The night was still on the mountains, though the day was not far off when they went down the hillside, and they could not see the glamour of the valley, but all the poetry and the sweet illusions of life were in their hearts. In April, when the hawthorn was white and the apple blossoms were bursting every hour, Lizzie Story became Mrs. Bertie E. Stein, and her great and unselfish love found at last its reward.

ESSIE DORTCH.

They call them "coon songs." Our new standard dictionary now defines the word "Coon" in one of its uses—"The Negro of the South." "The Wilson and Watkins Grand Opera Company." That is the way the flaring posters read on the bill board in Nashville, and I went to see and to hear the performance of the grand opera company when it came off. Why the arbiters of our language would fasten the term "coon" by the sanction of the dictionary on a worthy people, bringing them further into ridicule, though they are striving to do well against odds, is hard to determine, while those authorities of our tongue lay claim to generosity and respect for the significance of words in their passing upon them. They call them "Coon songs," and that is meant for Negro songs in this year of our Lord eighteen hundred and ninety-nine. There are songs, distinctly Negro songs—"the only native American music," so says the great composer, Devarak. What relation "Coon songs" bear to Negro melodies even so great a composer as Devarak could not tell, unless he could define the relation of chalk to cheese. Certainly, between these two, there is just as much relation as there is between Negro melodies and "Coon songs." And the performance of the Wilson and Watkins Grand Opera Company would be another thing. Davarak could not define musically in any relation to grand opera. But then it does not matter. Wilson and Watkins were a grand success. They had a large company, and they sang coon songs well. The cake-walk was fine. The buck dancing was superb. The opera had a plot, too, so it was given out, but I am certain I could never make out what it was, except in a general way, that it meant to bring the Negro up from his savagery in Africa through several hundred years of slavery in the United States, and then his freedom up to his present high degree of advancement. The affair ended up with a Negro on a throne, though crap-shooting, policy-playing and general horse play went on to the end and before the throne, while the king showed as much savagery and thieving propensities in all his courtly surroundings as was seen several hundred years back in the beginning of the opera. But it did not matter. Congruity and artistic effect were not to the point. The

168

coon songs were fine, and they are all the rage in this present day. The performance showed that the Negro had truly broken out in vaudeville, even if it were under the head of grand opera, and the fact that the Negro can draw such crowds of the white race to see him dance and to hear him sing, and can for the hour dispel all care, giving laughter and merriment in return, is a promise of better things to come and of a career before the footlights that will do much for the race by and by. But there was one in the audience who did not speculate upon the race's future, nor the philosophy of its connection with other things, but was charmed with the whole performance, and saw nothing but the highest art in it all, and whose awakened ambition filled her head with visions of glory for herself. Essie Dortch was from the country and was just finishing her first year in Fisk University. It had not been a very happy year for her, though she had never before been in such grand surroundings. Indeed, it was the superior surroundings that gave rise to her unhappiness. She was in the grades of the preparatory department of the school. She was a pretty girl certainly, but there were many such in Fisk University and who had far better advantages and therefore outshone Essie in all things. In the South the Negro in slavery times and immediately afterwards shared the aristocratic and social distinctions of the white families with whom they were connected. The Dortchs were the richest and most aristocratic family in Blyden. Martha Dortch, who had been lady's maid to Captain Dortch's wife, had the Dortch blood in her veins, and she was proud of this fact. When she was a free woman and mistress of her own house, she still paid due deference to her former white people, but she carried her head high above the people of her own race and kept Essie dressed like a fine lady. It was but natural that Essie, who in her own village was the prettiest girl, the most advanced in her books, and the idol of all the boys, should be unhappy when she found herself scarcely noticed in Fisk University society. She had gone to the school with some vague notions of improvement mentally, but flirtation and fanciful courtship heroics with the young men, where she would be the center of attraction in that far-famed institution of learning, had been the things uppermost in Essie's mind before she left. She had many times stood before her glass at home practicing bows and smiles and going through fanciful introductions which she remembered with biting humiliation at school. Early in May she was a little unwell and was sent to board in the city by the advice of a doctor who thought school boarding and confinement not good for this country girl. Now it happened that John Walters, the handsomest man in the Wilson and Watkins Grand Opera Company, came to board where Essie Dortch was staying. He was able at once to appreciate all her charms and laid seige to her heart with all fervor of his nature. Essie was vain, young and unsuspecting. Her school surroundings and dissatisfied frame of mind made her ready for the first snare spread for her. John Walters pointed out all the glories of their Grand Opera Company, and how she could win fame for herself if she would join them. Essie could not sing, but she was a beautiful dancer and up in all the "buck and wing" dancing of the country districts, and that was the kind of dancing for the Wilson and Watkins Opera Company. In all the Negro advancement which the company set forth, they had not got him up to skirt dancing, so that Essie in her art was ready for the stage at once. So that night when

171

she sat looking on, ambition was tugging hard at her heart, and what was more pitiful, love was growing in her breast for the rake who was playing false to her innocence and ignorance. But Essie was an upright girl in morals as far as she knew them, and this John Walters soon saw and acted accordingly. He played love to this simple country girl in the most approved manner, and told her of the glories of the road life until her head and heart were turned. The Wilson and Watkins Grand Opera Company closed their season at Nashville and disbanded until July, when they were to go down East for the watering places where they found summer engagements. When John Walters offered to engage himself to Essie she accepted him readily, but when he wished to take her to Cincinnati to await the reorganization of the company in July, she promptly refused and insisted that he should come out to her home and visit her to be regularly engaged and accepted by her parents. John objected to this, but when he found this same country girl ignorant of the world, but evidently accustomed to have her beaux do her bidding, he promised to come out the third week in June.

When Essie reached home her admirers

flocked around her, but she was full of airs
and soon let Aaron Dodd, whom she formerly favored above the others, know that
she was now looking higher than he was.
When John Walters came out with his fine
dressing and city airs, Aaron Dodd knew
at once that he stood no further chances
with Essie. In smoothness of tongue, general appearance and outside culture John
Walters met all of Martha Dortch's re-
quirements, but she let him know at once
that Essie could not go away with him to
join his company unless she was properly
married to him. He suggested that he
would be ready to marry in a year, and
hinted vaguely of his city property and of
his need for a mother-in-law to take care
of his home while he and his wife were on
the road. This hint appealed strongly to
Martha's ambition and desire for city
life and higher society, which she got a
glimpse of when she took Essie to Nashville to put her in school. But Martha
Dortch liked people to come to the point
and to speak out, therefore, when John
Walters said no more of that city prospect,
she became suspicious of his truthfulness
and treated him with much less warmth
when he called. But this John Walters
affected not to see and made daily calls on

Essie till that memorable Saturday came round that so turned the tide of affairs in Essie Dortch's life.

It was a gala day for Blyden and I recall with pleasure the picture of the village and the surrounding country as I saw it that day. West of the village there was a long line of blue hills rising and falling in beautiful undulations as they came down from the highland Rim of Middle Tennessee. The sun of a glorious June day was dropping down behind the hills and making way for a glorious June night. Diamond-stone Kitt was in the town selling Indian medicines, working his marvelous cures and giving cheap theatricals to a most appreciative country audience. On that night special features had been advertised. When long shadows began lengthening out over the hills and the shades of night to creep up the valley, the low rumble of wagon wheels, the neighing of horses, shouts and laughter of men and the tramping of crowds were heard in all directions coming over the hills, through the valley, woodland and lanes to the Saturday night performance of Diamond-stone Kitt. With heart-throbs of delicious pleasure Essie set out to the entertainment with John Walters. They walked leisurely down the lane and crossed a meadow where the air was filled with a damp scent of moss and ferns, and the breath of night was sweet. The air trembled with the croaking of frogs and shrill cries of Katy-dids. The Saturday night's performance was to wind up Diamond-stone Kitt's stay in the village and the people were eagerly looking for the extraordinary features that had been promised. Kitt had made Walter's acquaintance and engaged him to sing coon songs and to dance, and this he had announced through the country-side for miles around. Secretly Essie was pledged to dance with Walters, a thing her mother would not have permitted if she had known. The crowd filled the great tent early and ladies paid their dimes extra for front seats, as the aristocrats pay dollars for choice seats and boxes in fine theaters of the great cities. Diamond-stone Kitt put business first. He made his speech and told of the wonderful cures of his medicines. He understood human nature well. For instance, he would sell medicine for rheumatism for just so many minutes, and after that he would not sell the medicine for ten times its price. He allowed no time for indecision and making up the mind. Those perfectly well hearing his speech would be inclined to buy his medicine, and when the sale came on there was necessarily a rush to get the medicine with no time to consider the wisdom of it. The crowd would surge and push for it until the bell tapped. Then, he would bring forth a medicine for some other disease, and those who had not been able to get to him in time to get the medicine for rheumatism would buy the medicine for the next evil and so on to the end of the time allotted for the sale of cures. Then came the show. An acrobat came upon the stage first. He was a sight to see as he stood in the glow of the lamp light in his green scale-bespangled tights. His pitching the glittering balls and dangerously sharp knives in mid-air with such rapidity and dexterity amazed beyond words those slow-moving farm-worked men, who were only accustomed to handle the plow, the hoe and the rake with leisure-like movement. After the acrobat's performance, John Walters came upon the stage with his guitar and with all the airs of an ancient troubadore, but not to sing of the heroics of Homer, but of languishing love for Liza Lou. His sweet tenor voice rang out over the audience and thrilled it with such sweet singing as the most of them had never heard before.

When the songs were concluded, with all the pomp of the master of great ceremonies Diamond-stone Kitt introduced John Walters and Essie Dortch as partners for the fine dancing promised. There was a subdued murmur of surprise and admiration when Essie was led forward by Walters. She wore a white chalis with a broad belt of blue ribbon fluttering from her waist, and a narrow band of blue around her neck. She had a red rose in her hair and a bunch of purple clematis on her heaving young bosom. She looked in her wealth of youthful beauty as fresh as the morning, and in her movements she was as graceful as a fawn. Her eyes sparkled with excitement and intense pleasure. She knew all eyes were turned on her in admiration. Her exquisite quickening of a strong imagination gave her in that brief moment a taste of the life of passionate living for which she had been longing all her life. The impression of her own beauty was heightened by the presence of her handsome partner, who had with him the air of the city and refinement. At first they danced the measures of the country dance known on the stage as "buck and wing dancing." This

was familiar enough to those looking on,
but the same steps they were accustomed
to see done by the country louts were done
so gracefully by these two, it seemed to
them as if they were looking at a new kind
of dancing. At school Essie had learned
to waltz, and that was a form of dancing
many of those country people had never
seen. "Buck and wing dancing" suggest
free air, shady groves, saw-dust and all
the jollity of country life and picnics. And
what is still a more beautiful picture that
it brings to the mind is that of youthful
vigor, good health and strong animal life
necessary to the physical exertion of the
dance. But the waltz is another thing. It
gives at once the vision of the drawing-
room, magnificent apartments, dreamy music and all the grandeur that belongs to
the dancing of the "Four Hundred." When
the band struck up a waltz and Essie with
her partner began to move in the sensuous
maze of its rhythm there was the impression all around that she had a part in another life than that of the village to which
they all belonged, and none had a deeper
consciousness of this than Essie Dortch
herself. Her triumph for the evening was
complete, her cup of happiness was filled
to the rim. Her vanity needed nothing

more to make it complete. After the entertainment was over she and Walters walked home slowly. The full moon shed a subtle and fascinating beauty over everything, bleaching the green valleys and hills to gray mysteries and folding them in a thousand dreams. The night breezes fanned Essie's cheeks, and the dewy grass brushed her feet as they crossed again the meadow. The perfume of the wild honeysuckle was in the air and the cries of a million living things were in the night, and in Essie Dortch's soul there was for the hour the bliss of a paradise. The news of her dancing had reached home before her, and a storm of wrath met her at the door. Martha Dortch felt herself and Essie scandalized beyond bearing by Essie's conduct. She gave John Walters a bitter tongue lashing and ordered him from her door, and told him never to darken it again. Essie, in her great shame and humiliation over her mother's rudeness, began to remonstrate, but that so angered her mother she seized the riding whip and whipped Essie unmercifully until her father interfered and sent Essie to her room. Burning with shame and sore in heart and body, Essie lay across her bed undressed and wept the night away, but fully resolved to leave home forever. John Walters disappeared the next day, but not before he had managed secretly to send Essie a letter in which he urged her to leave home and join him at Shellmound on Monday. She wrote a few lines in reply and pledged herself to join him as he asked. She kept in her room all day Sunday, and Martha, who had repented her violence of the night before, did not trouble her. Late in the afternoon her father came into the room, and brought her up some dinner. He was not a man who talked much, but Essie always understood him and loved him better than she did her mother, though it was her mother who influenced her most. She felt a sudden pang of heart because of the secret in it, knowing well the grief it would bring her father, who in his silent way had never given her anything but the tenderest love. When he turned to leave the room she clung to him and wept. He tried to comfort her and to make some excuse for her mother. He little dreamed that Essie's tenderness to him was a farewell.

The next morning when Essie stole down stairs and out of the house the moon was still shining, but away to the east the night was yielding to the day-break. Very soon there were long stretches of crimson that make you think of the palaces of the mother of roses, while away to the west there were banks of pale sea-green that the July dawn slowly drove away towards the Pacific. An hour after sunrise Essie had reached Liberty Hill, the last prominent and rugged spur of the hills from the southern part of the State that run northward to the valley of the Cumberland. At that point the abrupt hills that characterize the southern part of the State break off and to the north lies a gentle and lovely plain which stretches on for fifty miles to the banks of the Cumberland. As far as the eye could reach there were visions of green meadows and of fields ripe with golden wheat. There were dark stretches of woodland and here and there were farm houses almost hidden by their luxuriant gardens and orchards. Essie had viewed this lovely picture a thousand times, but its sublime beauty she had never felt before. There came into her heart a sudden sense of regret, for the sight of the valley brought her unexpectedly to a full sense of the sadness of farewell. For a moment she was tempted to turn back, but swiftly the thought of her punishment and shame returned and filled her heart anew with bitterness and resentment. So she walked on her journey until she came to the post-office at Four Corners, where she took the stage for Shellmound, which place she reached at noon. John Walters was waiting for her and secretly exulting over the turn of affairs which worked so much in his favor. But a little surprise was in store for him. Essie had had all the long morning for silent reflection, and she had reached one conclusion from which Walters could not move her. She told him that she had come that far to meet him, as she had promised, but that she would go no further unless she were married to him. He was not prepared for this, but he soon saw there was no other alternative, and finally agreed to a secret marriage, giving as his reason for this that he would be dismissed from the company by the manager if it were known that he was married. This contract did not fully meet Essie's desire, but she consented to it, as he promised to leave the company in a year. Early that night Elder Jones, a man of very pious demeanor, came to their stopping place, according to John Walter's request. He was given a paper purporting to be a marriage license, which he looked at critically through his gold-rimmed glasses and then pompously performed a marriage ceremony. That such a performance could be a sham from beginning to end never entered the trusting mind of Essie Dortch. In a few hours Mr. and Mrs. Walters were speeding along through the night on the train. They were going to join their Grand Opera Company at the watering places down East.

CHAPTER II.

The Wilson and Watkins Grand Opera Company went through its summer season at the various points on the sea shore, and in October the bill boards in Baltimore announced a week's performance of this highly successful company. Essie Dortch had found the life rough in some ways, but the predictions of John Walters as to her glory had come true. She was the most beautiful girl in the company. When she ran upon the stage in her pink satin dress with its spangles and ribbons and white slippers, she was loudly applauded. She was one of the popular attractions and her great vanity was ever gratified. John Walters was faithful and loving all through those bright summer days down by the sea. All her life Essie had lived in dreams, dreams of passionate living full of courtships, loving and being loved, and now her dreams were come true. There was only one secret regret and that was the fact that she could not let it be known that she was the wife of John Walters, that this handsome and beloved man was hers. One night just before time to start to the Opera House, early in the week of the company's run in Baltimore, when Belle Banks, her most intimate friend, told her that she should not be so open in her intimacy with John Walters, Essie confided the secret of their marriage. Then Belle told her that John Walters was already a married man and had three children, and if he had gone through any ceremony with her it was a sham one. Essie did not faint, nor cry, nor rave. An expression of hardness and horror spread over her young face.

"Do you know this to be true, Belle?" she said quietly.

"I do; we are from the same town. I know his wife and children."

Then Belle advised Essie to be quiet about the matter as the best way to avoid bringing herself into unnecessary scandal. Belle was used to the loose ways and the life of most people in the shows on the road, and saw no tragedy in Essie's situation. Essie's quietness led her to suppose that the girl did not take the matter much to heart, but she had little conception of the real character of Essie Dortch. At the bottom of all her vanity and shallowness of heart there was a prejudice and general pride of life and a teaching from her mother since childhood of the estimate of the Dortch blood and connection well calculated to save Essie from a low life. When the others went to the Opera House she remained behind unnoticed. All through the long hours of the singing, dancing and general horse play of the company's performance she sat alone in her lodging place with a growing fire of resentment in her heart that promised no good for John Walters. She was not missed at first, but the manager was very angry when it came her time to dance and it was found that she was absent. Walters, who was regarded as somewhat responsible for her, came back to their lodging place in no good humor. Without delay or ceremony she told him what Belle Banks had told her, and asked him if it were true. He saw at once that she could be no longer deceived, and assuming a great bravado attempted to crush her at once, and told her it was true. She stood up before him and faced him with eyes that made his craven heart flinch.

"John Walters, I have lived straight all

my life. You came to me with a lying
tongue and a lying heart and told me that
you loved me. I loved you back, not only
enough to run away from my home and my
parents for you, but enough to have died
for you. I could have had the pick of all
the boys in Blyden, but I put them all under my feet as so much trash for you, and
for this you have made me a common woman. What did you do it for?"

"Well, if I did, what are you going to do
about it," he replied.

"What am I going to do about it? This."

Her hand suddenly shot out from under
her cloak and by the time a gleam of something in it made an impression on the re-
tina of his insolent eye, John Walters felt
something in his side like red hot iron, and
following the gleam there was a flash of
many stars and in his ears the rush of
mighty waters, and then there was darkness and oblivion.

Between mid-night and day the bell rang
at the convent of the Sisters of Mercy and
a girl in pink satin and dancing slippers
was in this most worldly gear taken before
the mother superior, to whom she told her
story and asked to be taken in from the
world. And while she made her confession,
John Walters lay in a lodging house at the

point of death, but Essie Dortch was not a murderess, as she had told the holy mother superior she was.

The Grand Opera Company, after its week in Baltimore, went its way, while Essie Dortch, its popular dancer, in a nun's cell did penance and learned the first lessons of the anchorite.

At Blyden, the fall passed away and winter and spring in their turn and once more it was summer, and Aaron Dodd especially thought of Essie with the season. Her father and mother bore their sorrow, each in their own way. Martha Dortch felt a secret remorse for rashness with her child, but she had her pride to sustain and to keep her head still above the neighbors, upon whom she had always looked down. She therefore affected indifference about Essie's running away. She took pains, however, to give it out that Essie was married to the man with whom she ran off. Essie wrote of the marriage as soon as it took place. When some who were glad to see Martha taken down expressed a doubt about the marriage, Aaron Dodd went to Shellmound and to the house where Essie was married. When he came home, he silenced all tongues who were casting evil reproaches on the woman he loved.

Essie Dortch.

Sampson Dortch, or "Uncle Sampson," as he was called by white and black, was a silent man, saying but little at most times, but he grew even more silent after Essie's departure. There grew just the faintest shadow of reserve between him and Martha. He never uttered one word of blame for her harshness towards Essie, but he felt it, and Martha knew he felt it. It irritated her and made her fretful and quarrelsome at times. But it takes two to quarrel, and Uncle Sampson was not a quarrelsome man. His mouth and eyes told that, for his dark eyes were like those you see in the hind of the forest, and his mouth was all tenderness—a weak mouth they call it, I believe. He had the mouth and eyes that are ever a true sign of a heart that can ache and suffer in silence. Nobody ever knew how that silent and uncouth country man suffered while he worked his life away in the fields at the plow. There was something pathetic in the awarkwardness of his efforts to cultivate Essie's flowers in the early mornings before he went to his labor in the field. The hoe was at home in his hands, but the vigorous blows upon the bushes, briars and weeds were the accustomed handling. But the love of the heart is a great teacher, and in time there came gentleness and caressing in the stirring of earth about Essie's flowers. Her merigolds, bachelor's buttons, zenias, life-everlasting, Sweet William, geraniums and roses grew in all the rioting life of spring and blossomed in the profusion of summer. The bees came buzzing lazily among them and then went their way with their harvest of honey. If the flowers ever wondered what had become of Essie, they never asked the silent old man who attended them in her stead. If they had, he could not have told them, for no word came to him of his run-away child. One day in December, more than two years after Essie's elopement, Aaron Dodd went to Shellmound with a load of wheat, and while passing through one of the streets saw an announcement that made his heart leap. ''The Wilson and Watkins Grand Opera Company, December third and fourth, at the Buckingham Theater.'' It was the second night's performance, and Aaron thanked God in his heart that he came to town that day. Long before the opening hour he was at the door of the theater, and when at last the performance began, Aaron waited with a surging heart for the appearance of Essie Dortch. There was the usual exhibition of the race development as shown through the events of the centuries and through slavery in this country, but the development shown two years before was somewhat curtailed on this occasion. There was, of course, the indispensable "coming all the way down the line," but the greatest effort was to set forth the present day attainment. Would you believe it, after two years, the Wilson and Watkins Grand Opera Company reappeared with two skirt dancers. This was advancement indeed. Now it happens that skirt dancing is not a matter of movement of the legs and feet, but the performance of a contortionist. There must be many yards of the finest silk, calcium and electric lights and a woman with arms well enough trained to wave the silk folds in all possible whirls in the electric light, changing the skirt to all hues to get the fantastic and poetic effect of the present day skirt dance. The Wilson and Watkins Grand Opera Company had neither the light nor the trained contortionist, so the skirt dance was only the regular "buck and wing" species, with a few flirts and whirls of silk yards added. The dance would have been well enough under its own name, but was ridiculous out of it.

Aaron Dodd waited in vain for Essie Dortch to appear, and at the close of the performance he went at once behind the scenes. The first person he met was Bill Cowden, the wide-mouthed and white-eyed performer who played the plantation Negro in the opera.

"Where is Essie Dortch? This is the company she went away with?"

"Essie who? Dar ain't no gal uv dat denomination in dis here show," replied Bill, still in his stage language and swager. But one of the singers who was in the company with Essie heard Aaron's question and told him her story, and added, "We think she went to the sisters in the convent at Baltimore, but when the police sought her there for stabbing John Walters the nuns denied that Essie had joined them."

Aaron went home with a disappointed and sore heart, but fully resolved to hunt for Essie till he found her, if it took the rest of his life. He was occupied the next two months in selling out his farm produce and arranging his affairs so that he could leave home for a short or long time, as the occasion might require. He had kept the secret of his love and desolate heart to himself. He and Essie's father had grown close together because of a love and a grief alike in their hearts. Sampson Dortch felt Aaron's keen sympathy without knowing the sequel to it. Aaron went away on his journey without telling any one of its purpose. He did not know where nor in what condition he should find Essie, and thought it best to be silent. He had never traveled far, and Baltimore was a long way off for him, but love was at the end of the long journey drawing him and shortening the distance. When he reached Baltimore he sought the colored convent at once, expecting to find Essie, but was once more doomed to bitter disappointment. The sisters were suspicious at first, and withheld the information he wanted, but Aaron Dodd was a young man even strangers would not mistrust long. He was finally told all about Essie, and that she was then in the Convent of the Holy Family at New Orleans. It was a sore disappointment to find himself over a thousand miles from the one he so anxiously sought and seven hundred miles farther away than when he was at home, but there was the comfort of knowing at last exactly where she was. He fell in with some sailors and learned from them that he could get a chance to work his way as a deck-hand on a New Orleans steamer. The steamer went to Philadelphia before it

started for New Orleans, and the two weeks
Aaron passed in waiting were hard to pass
over. But at last the great steamer, having
been reloaded, headed south and put to sea.
The deck-hand experience was a rough one
for Aaron, but he passed through it and six
weeks after leaving home he landed in New
Orleans. It was Saturday night when he
reached the city, and early next morning
he found out what he wanted to know
about the Holy Family of the Colored Sisters of Charity. He crossed Jackson
Square and passed by the old Saint Louis
Cathedral and turned into Orleans Alley
which lies between the Cathedral and the
Cabildo. Passing by Royal street, the alley
widens into Orleans Street, and midway
the first block Aaron Dodd came to the
Convent of the Holy Family. He was ignorant of the great change that had come
over that quiet building and of all the romance and unique history that slumbers
in that most interesting spot. Indeed, this
convent was long ago the theater of New
Orleans, where great actors once stirred
the passions of men and singers noted in
their day thrilled audiences with their music. But that which is most romantic of
the place is the history of the far-famed
quadroon balls which took place here away

back in the days when the Nineteenth Century was young, and when Cables Madame Delphine was a character of importance. It was Easter morning when Aaron Dodd came to the place. He did not know much about the celebration of that annual festival. In the country district where he lived he had seen only one commemoration of the day, and that service had been rather confusing in its bearing. The minister who had never seen the inside of a college and had had only a few short sessions in the district school in his boyhood did the best he knew. He preached from the book of Esther, which he pronounced Easter. The ladies of the church, who had seen pictures of little chickens bursting from the shells of eggs, connected the idea of the day with the poultry yard in some vague way, and many hens' nests were made in the church and filled with hard-boiled eggs painted in various colors. The eggs were given the children of the Sunday School. A young college student, who was in the neighborhood for a day or so, attended the service, and was asked to say a few words. He did not wish to reveal the minister's ignorance and did not say much, but told them in a few words that the day celebrated the resurrection of Christ and the promise of new

194

life. Aaron and most of the others went from the service rather confused, and he had never seen any other celebration of Easter. So in New Orleans he came to the day of that glorious festival with only the thought of Essie Dortch in mind. But a wonderful sight was awaiting him in the services of the convent, once the theater of New Orleans. He saw no array of Creole dancers whose memory is inseparable from the place, but he did see that which was almost as unique—many black-robed sisters of mercy of the Negro race. Instead of the blare of bands for the dancers, whose feet have long since gone from the dance to the tomb, he heard the Te Deum and the Gloria. Aaron Dodd, who had all his life been used to a simple service of song and prayer, followed by an exciting discourse by the preacher in charge, was filled with a sense of holy awe by the pomp and magnificent ritualistic service. The sisters came in so reverently and silently along the aisles he heard nothing except the faintest rattle of beads and rustle of their garments as they knelt with folded hands in prayer and then sank into their seats. There was, however, quite a stir when the boys and girls, pupils of the Academy and Saint Peter's Asylum, came in, pausing in the aisles before the images of Christ with that swift bending of the knee and fluttering of the fingers crossing themselves before they took their seats. With this group of young Catholic worshipers came Sister Beatrice. Her face was still young and beautiful, but from it all expression of vanity and pride of life had gone out, leaving behind a stamp of sorrow and meek submission. The beautiful young Sister Beatrice robed in black, with her pale face encased in white, was Essie Dortch.

On Monday Aaron Dodd called at the convent to see her, and until she saw him she thought she was a murderess, and her relief was great when she learned that she did not kill John Walters that fearful night in Baltimore. Aaron thought when she knew the facts in the case Essie would be ready to come home, for he had not dreamed that she was in the convent for any other purpose than to hide, but he was mistaken. She listened quietly to Aaron's plea and pent-up love confession and wept a little—perhaps because of the stirring up of memories of past things of the heart for this man whom she knew to be good and true, but whose love she could not reward. She had sought the convent in Baltimore as a home of refuge, but her vow and the devotion and religious life of the convent were real to her now. The ritualistic and pictorial service of the Catholic Church were well calculated to appeal to a nature like hers. All the intensities and sentimental emotions of her girlhood had found an outlet in the Catholic religion and in the activities in the sisterhood of mercy. She sent messages of love to her parents and bade Aaron Dodd an affectionate good-bye. He sorrowfully turned his face to the north and to the Highland Rim of Middle Tennessee—his home, but home never to be quite the same again. In the Crescent City, the queen of the cities of the South, Aaron Dodd left all the romance of his life and the one great desire and hope of his soul behind him forever and forever.

THE DEATH OF HANOVER.

It was at McGrathiana in the midst of the beautiful Blue Grass region of Kentucky, that Hanover, the leading thoroughbred sire of America, was put to death. Gangrene had set in from an injured foot, and after a council of leading veterinarians it was decided that in mercy the great stallion should be put to death.

The news went over the wires in all directions; for Hanover, though but a horse, was world-wide famous. He had been in this world fifteen years, and that begins to be a long time in horse life. He was sired by Hindoo, out of Bourbon Belle, by Imp. Bonnie Scotland. He left Clay and Woodford at their Runnymede Stud on one of their annual sales of yearlings, and went away merely as a chance promise and a hope of his new masters, the Dwyer Bros.

From the very first on the race course he was king of the turf, and in a short time won for his owners, in stakes and purses, the enormous sum of one hundred and twenty thousand dollars.

Early in his career he had trouble with the left foot, which his owners had nerved to keep him on the track. But that treatment failed in its purpose and was destined in the end to lead to Hanover's tragical death. After a brief reign in his marvelous flights on the race course he was ruled out of his kingdom, and for fifteen thousand dollars went to a new master at McGrathiana Stud.

Here was the beginning of new glory. In seven years seventy-four of his progeny were sent to the turf, where they faced the starter and won half a million. And thus Hanover, in all avenues of horse glory, surpassed the records of all American horses, not excepting the great Lexington himself. A well known authority said of him: "Viewed from any standpoint, Hanover seems to be the Stockwell of his day, the sire pre-eminent of his country and time." Now all of this is big talk and high-flown phrases just about a horse, it seems to me, but such were the dispatches that went over the wires, and people read them with interest.

Indeed, it is true that even, as men who have pedigrees and get into their keeping large sums of money, even when the manner of getting is dubious, a kingly race horse has respect paid to him that other horses cannot have, although they may drug all their life long in hauling and carrying the burdens of men to and fro, and in that way facilitate commerce, increase the general wealth, advance civilization and national glory; but all the time are thought of only as beasts of burden, fit only for beating, thankless toil and often half starvation, while the likes of Hanover are pampered and spoken of in terms of respect. But that is the way of the world, and the lot of the serving beast of burden— in some measure it is the lot of some men. Yet, I have no quarrel to make with the world nor with men and least of all with hightoned horses like Hanover.

He had his glory and his retinue of servants, but there is no evidence that he was unduly proud or that he thought more highly of himself than he ought. He was just a horse, enjoyed his pleasant surroundings, the green meadows of the springtime, the soft sunshine and blue skies of old Kentucky. But there is one evil which no flesh can escape—sickness and death spare none. Honors, pedigrees and length of purse fail all alike in the settlement of the last accounts.

Hanover had a severe spell of indigestion and came near to death. For weeks he had to be fed with a force pump, but in time he rallied and came out of his shadow of the valley of death—and came out hungry. He had to be sparingly fed lest he should over-eat himself in his feeble condition. In this precaution Hanover was like some men who have been pampered all their lives, who never had to go hungry nor forego a single want which money could buy. He became impatient and grew angry. Even so great a horse as Hanover was denied the privilege of speech; so he could not curse and swear and order his servants about—that is, he could not do it in ordinary English. Perhaps he did it in his way, for he neighed, kicked and pawed wrathfully in his stall, and the pawing proved his ruin.

That luckless left foot which forced him from the glory of the turf was bruised and having been nerved, the veterinarians could not get it to heal. The council decided that he must die by degrees if left to himself, and a merciful death was recommended. Dr. Bryan was sent for to come up from Lexington to McGrathiana. It was early morning when he arrived— one of those beautiful mornings that one sometimes sees and feels in old Kentucky early in the spring. The sky was all blue and the sunshine soft. The air still had in it the breath of March. It was one of those mornings when the last suggestion of winter takes its farewell in a backward glance at the approaching spring maiden, whose gentle presence and enchanting spell were fallen on beautiful McGrathiana. That elusive beauty which hides in soft tones and faint colors on bare fields and stripped copses was everywhere apparent. The lilac buds were swollen and showed the first faint touches of color promised in things to come. Soft lights played over the meadows and caressed the delicate hues of Kentucky blue grass, beginning to come forth abundantly from the dark bed, where it had slept under January snows, dreaming of the upper air.

There was a friendly power passing between the earth and the sky and faint breathing of new life about to awake in new glory. The dawn of the resurrection had come. But oh! it was all different in Hanover's stall. He was in pain and could not understand what seem to be such sudden and base desertion.

When Dr. Bryan arrived the master of McGrathiana was nowhere to be found, nor any of his family. The Doctor was puzzled at first, for all of the stable hands were gone, too. He waited half an hour for sight of the master and directions. But, finally, the pitiful truth dawned upon him. The master of McGrathiana with his family and those rough stable hands had all fled. They could not bear to see Hanover die. In the moments of his triumph at the race course the master, the retinue of servants, with all that fickle throng ready to shout for the one that wins, no matter which, had followed him with glad hurrahs and exulting cheer on cheers.

Afterwards, in a more quiet life of glory and becoming dignity, a whole retinue of servants had ever been ready to give attention and serve Hanover, the horse king. But, in his last moments of pain and when the hour of death was come, they all forsook him and fled—no, not quite all. There was one old Negro, who something like another servant long ago, halted around the corner at some distance. When Dr. Bryan saw him he called him up and said: "Well, Oscar, where are the folks?"

"Deys all gone, boss. I recon' you and me will hafter—" He did not finish the sentence and Dr. Bryan understood.

"All right, Oscar, come along."

The old Negro had passed through all of the sorrows of slavery, the bitter issues of the war and the hardships of his thirty years of freedom, but, perhaps, in all of his life he had never felt keener pangs at heart than at that moment when he shuffled behind the doctor towards the stables. Hanover, with all the keen sensibilities of a noble horse, had felt his neglect, and when the doctor and old Oscar appeared he whinnied with that peculiar whinny half of glad welcome and half of reproach that a horse will make when in pain or fright and some well known friend appears.

Doctor Bryan began at once to put the chloroform bag over his head and old Oscar tried to assist him. Perhaps it was because the hard toil of many years and the rheumatism of many winters had so stiffened his fingers that they were only a clumsy hindrance to Dr. Bryan; and, too, his old eyes were weak, so he said: "You will hatter 'scuse me, boss, my eyes is allers weak when the wind blows, I can't see what I's doin'," he said as he turned away. Dr. Bryan did not think to mention the fact that the wind was not blowing then. Indeed, this man who was so used to work in blood and death, as a matter of fact, when he saw the stream of water coursing down that old weatherbeaten and black face, his own eyesight was not so good as usual, and the nose took on several coatings of red. And Hanover, who in all of his life had never had anything but kind treatment, was all unsuspicious.

He thought this new kind of a halter put all over his head and the unusual proceedings were in some way meant for his good, and he submitted patiently. Still, there was something about that bag that did not smell good; and soon the thing began to stifle and he shook his head impatiently; but matters got worse and worse. His breath came hard and a keen sense of fright ran through his heart; he began to struggle and wonder where his old friend Oscar was, and why he did not come to his relief. He sent out a little distressing neigh to him one last little choking call for help. The old Negro heard and understood that call. His eyesight got worse and his hearing became defective and he ran around the corner that the doctor might not hear an eruption which could not proceed from the eyes.

With this flight of the last of the old retinue Hanover was deserted. That strange white man with the new kind of halter rewarded his hard struggles only by putting more of the vile-smelling stuff into the bag. But, somehow, it began to get easier. The pain in his foot all went away. Bit by bit

he forgot all about things—forgot all about
the exhileration in his swift flight on the
race course, the crack of the jockey's whip
and the deafening cheer of the multitude
when he was the first to run his nose under
the wire at the finish of the stretch. He
forgot all about his friends and ceased to
wonder where they had gone. It did not
matter—nothing mattered now. He was
too sleepy to think any more and laid down
on the straw in his stall.

Old Oscar blew a horn just as they used
to do in slavery time. From the back side
of the farm a few other Negroes came in.
Now, to the Negro mind, there is nothing
like a marriage, a cake walk and a funeral.
The mid-week prayer-meetings in the
churches don't go for much, except with a
few of the amen-corner brothers and sisters, although the Negroes are said to be
very religious.

In most of the churches the crowd is slim
at the eleven o'clock services on Sundays.
They got used to letting the white folks go
at that hour in slavery times while they
staid at home and did the work, and then
they did their church-going at night. It
has now been more than thirty years of
freedom, but force of habit is strong. Cake
walks have somewhat fallen in disrepute

among the better element, especially since the white people have taken up the entertainment as one more disparaging take-off on the Negroes. Still, a cake walk can yet get a good house, and a church is scarcely ever large enough to hold the crowd at a wedding. And funerals—these are the chiefest of all—especially if the dead belonged to the Masons, or the Odd Fellows, or the Household of Ruth, or the Sons and Daughters of the Morning, and so on ad-infinitum—no matter what sort of an order.

The crowd will go for hours beforehand, fill the seats of the church and line the streets for a block on the outside. There will be a procession of tall feathers, men with gold-worked aprons, women with long purple robes and the Grand Princess herself will be in her robe and crown, with every trace of Mis' Julie's cook at breakfast obliterated; and O! glory, there will be a brass band. And yet, a sight of all that magnificence is only a part of the funeral which draws. The Negroes are above all things loving-hearted and emotional, and perhaps nowhere else can their depths of feeling be so stirred with a mingling of grief and anticipated happiness as in the presence of death, where the pictures of heaven and hell are so held up by the preacher in charge. When that handful of Negro servants had made beautiful a new mound of earth at McGrathiana they could not relieve themselves of the feeling that they were acting at a great funeral. And they were at a little loss to know what to do, till young Abe Jones, an aspirant to become an exhorter in the Zion Methodist Church, took off his old hat and began to break the solemn silence with that half chant and half moan that all Negroes know about in the fashion of giving out the hymns, two lines at a time—"And am I born to die, and lay this body down."

Then that soulful gift of song—that heartfelt gift of song, in which the Negroes excel all men in all lands, moving hearts with pathos unutterable—went out under the blue sky and over that new mound of earth and the bare fields round about.

In all that region Brer. Jerry is known to be powerful in prayer. When the song was over they all knelt down on dear mother earth, who had just opened her bosom to take to her breast one more of her children, who, to those simple-hearted and sorrowful men now under the full emotion of the funeral, was no longer a horse, but an earthly being, who, like themselves, must at last go back to the great mother of us all.

So Bro. Jerry prayed, and in his fervor brought down the very throne of God, and there on his knees walked the golden streets of Jerusalem, as only the Negroes can do in their imagination on funeral occasions. To the very last Hanover, the great, was honored as became his achievements and world-wide fame.